# Virginia Fantastic

## Flash Fiction from the Old Dominion

### Edited by James Blakey

Whitaker Lyon Press

# Praise for *Virginia Fantastic*

***VIRGINIA FANTASTIC*** is exactly that: a fantastic and fantastical romp across the state with flash fiction set in some of the Old Dominion's most famous—and infamous—places. Whether weird or wacky, eerie or downright spooky, these short stories will have you casting a side eye the next time you visit a cavern, tour a Civil War battlefield, or take a stroll through Colonial Williamsburg.

**—Heather S. Cole, Author of *Virginia's Presidents***


***VIRGINIA FANTASTIC*** offers glimpses into 41 tantalizing magical and mythical worlds—some charming, some horrifying, some creepy, some thrilling. Some transport you to the future, while others are rooted in the deep past. But the common thread through all of them is they will make you look at the commonwealth with just a bit more wonder.

**—Beth Ford, Author of *Love Across Time***

# Praise for the Fantastic Anthologies

After having read *SHENANDOAH FANTASTIC*, I'll never see the Shenandoah Valley the same way again. Lurking around familiar sights—from local golf courses to ballfields to churches to mountains to lakes to Blackfriars Playhouse and Interstate 81—are the unfamiliar, sometimes humorous, often spooky, and occasionally baffling people and plots, twists and turns, that shine in this delightful collection.

—Evan Friss, *New York Times* Bestselling Author of *The Bookshop*

An endearing and absolutely Appalachian story. If you're in the mood for charming dialogue, and some adventure, this is your book!

—The Staunton Wallcrawler

By turns spooky, playful, and downright chilling, *CHARLOTTESVILLE FANTASTIC* laces its speculative stories with a touch of Southern charm. Whether you're in the mood for cursed books or deadly time loops, helpful ghosts or Bigfoot sightings, there's something for every fan of the supernatural in its pages.

—Katharine Schellman, Author of *Last Call at the Nightingale*

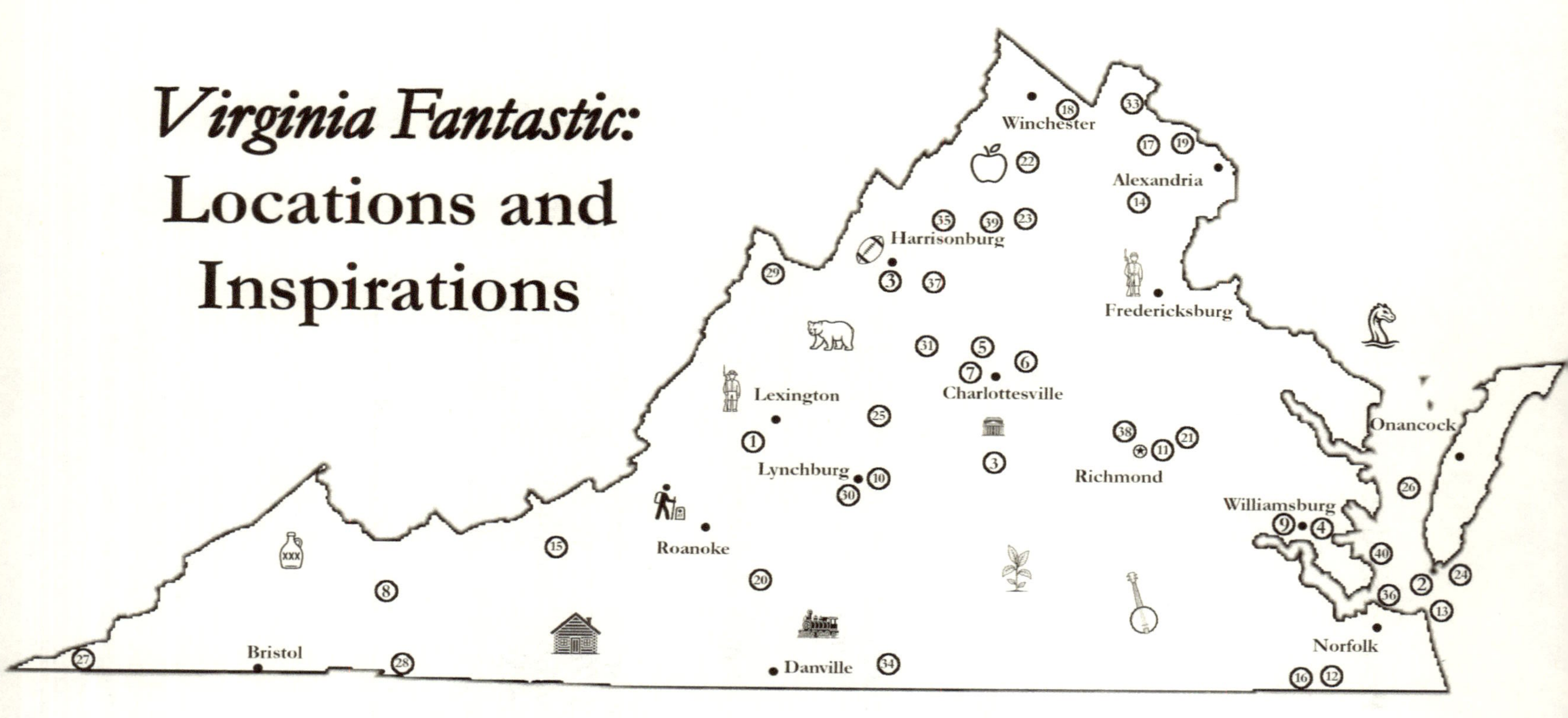

Virginia Fantastic: Locations and Inspirations
Winchester
Alexandria
Harrisonburg
Fredericksburg
Onancock
Lexington
Charlottesville
Richmond
Williamsburg
Lynchburg
Roanoke
Norfolk
Bristol
Danville

# THE STORIES



∞ Sovereign Battlestate Virginia

Library of Congress Control Number: 2026904575

ISBN: 979-8-9909340-6-1 (Paperback)

Whitaker Lyon Press

4464 North Pointe Drive

Broadway VA 22815

WhitakerLyon.com

*"I find nothing anywhere else... which Virginia need envy."*


—Thomas Jefferson—

# Contents

# Please Remain on the Marked Path

## JON NEGRONI

THE NATURAL BRIDGE TOUR takes forty-five minutes if no one asks about Thomas Jefferson or other mythical creatures. I know this because I've walked it three times a day for seven years, long enough to memorize where people stop for photos and where they pretend to listen. On Thursdays, however, I have to adjust the route. Because on Thursdays, the Natural Bridge hosts Unnatural Weddings.

I tell the group it's a partial closure. Maintenance. Safety checks. Everyone nods like they understand and then immediately steps over the rope anyway. I herd them back with my clipboard and my voice, which I've learned to keep calm. The Bridge prefers calm tones.

The stone arch rises where it always has, perfectly natural. Water trickles through the gorge below, louder than it looks. This is the part where people usually gasp. Today they don't. The humidity has taken the fight out of them.

"Please remain on the marked path," I say. "And if you hear anything unusual, that's just the acoustics."

This is untrue, but it is close enough.

The Snallygaster arrives early, which is typical. He circles once above the arch, wings beating the air into a dry, metallic wind that smells like rust and old feathers. A woman in a JMU hat points up and asks, "Is that a drone?"

"No," I say, without looking. "Please remain on the marked path."

The Snallygaster settles on the far side of the gorge, talons scraping stone. He is dressed formally, as requested. The ribbon tied around his neck is black and already fraying. He gnaws on it anyway. Nerves.

Chessie is late.

To be fair, though, Chessie's always late. Water-bound beings dislike schedules, and Chessie has come a long way from Chesapeake Bay for her wedding.

I check my watch, then my clipboard, then the sky. Sunset's still an hour out, but the light's already slanting. We don't have much time. I begin the history portion early to buy some. I talk about limestone and erosion and the years it takes for a thing to look permanent. People like that part. It makes them feel patient by association.

A boy at the back tugs on his father's sleeve. "Why's it so windy down here?"

"Natural funneling," I say. "Please remain on the marked path."

The first sign of Chessie is the *damp*. Not rain—she hates rain—but a creeping wetness that slicks the stones and darkens the moss. The air thickens. The trickle below swells, then settles, like the Bridge itself is adjusting.

I clear my throat.

Chessie rises from the gorge in sections, which is the only polite way to do it. A curve of dark water. A suggestion of scales. The sense of something very old checking its reflection in the stone. She's not dressed. She's never seen the point.

The Snallygaster croons, low and reedy. Chessie answers with a sound like tide tables being torn in half.

"Alright," I say, clapping once. "We're going to pause here."

A man with a camera raises it. I step into his line of sight.

"No photos," I say. "Park policy."

"Of the rock?" he asks.

"Of anything," I say, and smile until he lowers it.

The vows are written phonetically on my clipboard. I've memorized them, but the clipboard matters. Objects matter. I step into the space beneath the arch and sense the pressure shift, subtle as a headache coming on.

The Snallygaster bows deeply. Chessie does not bow at all. They have rehearsed this. We all have.

"We are gathered," I begin, "because this is the only place where air and water can agree."

The Bridge hums, just barely. It always does at this part.

I keep my voice steady. I don't look at either of them directly. Witnessing is not the same as seeing, and humans like me confuse the two.

Behind me, the boy laughs. I raise a hand without turning.

"Please remain on the marked path."

The Snallygaster hesitates on the third vow. This is also typical. Commitment is hard when you molt. His wings shudder, stirring grit. The Bridge tightens, just a hair.

"Continue," I say.

He does.

Chessie's response is quieter, a pull instead of a push. The water below us surges, then calms.

The boy gasps. I risk a glance over my shoulder. He's staring straight at Chessie, mouth open, wonder all over his face.

"No," I say, sharper than I mean to. "Eyes on me, kid."

His father pulls him back. Good man.

The final vow requires a witness. It always does. I've stood in this place more times than I can count, holding other people's unions together with my voice and the Bridge's patience. I know how it feels when it works. I know how it feels when it doesn't.

"Do you accept," I say, and pause just long enough for the echo to finish.

They do. Both of them. Not perfectly. It's never perfect.

The Bridge yawns. The wind drops. The damp recedes. The Snallygaster lets out a sound of... joy? Chessie sinks back into the gorge, already tugging at him, already rearranging the currents of his life.

I step back onto the path.

"Well," I say to the group, "thank you for your patience."

"What was that?" someone asks.

"An acoustic phenomenon," I say. "Please remain on the marked path."

# Hope is a Thing with Brittle Scales

## EMBER BROOKS

IN A BAY GUARDED by capes of faraway kings, Merya sang to the sea and the things that it carried.

She hummed to blue crabs as she sealed her scales over cracks in their shells. She trilled to barnacles as she drifted over their beds, and she chanted to shads as she swam them upstream. Attuned to each life in the waters, she sang as the world spun from one age to the next.

She was singing when the first ships sliced through the waves, carrying a colony of pale new faces to shore, casting shadows across the sand. There had been more of her kind then, tilting their long necks back to gaze at the surface. Before the boats overhead turned from rounded wood to sharp-edged metal—became ferries and freighters and frigates. Before the water became murky and cloying, stinging the skin beneath her scales. Before her sisters abandoned their burrows in search of clearer waters.

For many tides, she longed to follow them. But if she went, what would become of the bass and blue crabs? The otters and oysters? Her kin had long guarded these waters, and she vowed not to be the last, even as her lungs shriveled, her scales brittled, and her gills curled and spasmed beneath algal darkness.

So Merya endured, while the rivers swept in sediments that burned and choked. She wound her body deep into spoiled sand, where she might regrow the scales she had given to patch shells. It would be a slow healing, in a sea so suffocated. But she hoped the water would bring her what she needed, as it always had before. When it did, she would wake and sing again.

And so Merya slept.

Then came the digging, shaking her awake. She shot from her burrow like a mackerel, hearts pounding and fins quaking. She did not—*could not*—sing as a long metal arm collapsed her warren of tunnels. As beams sank through the waves and impaled the sea floor. As a hollow snake was laid into the trench by parts, its huge, curving slabs settling into the place where she and her sisters once slumbered. And then, when every part had been pressed together, the noise began, a dull, endless droning through the shallows.

At first, Merya could not find her own song through the sound. She buried herself deep in the sand in search of quiet. She escaped to estuaries but could not stay away from the bay. She tried to bring the song back with her but could not hold onto it against the droning discord. She resolved again to endure.

Exhausted, she sank and let her sinuous body drape across the tunnel, scales scraping on cement. She let the sound shudder up her spine and throb through her veins.

After long hours, she began to hum with it, resonant and reverberating. As the pounding dissonance between them resolved, smaller sounds—voices, laughter, thin strains of music—seeped through the concrete. She sighed, slipping back into the sand to rest and restore her sickly scales.

And so Merya slept.

Then came the winter wind, whipping freezing whitecaps and ripping ships from their mooring. Anchors carved deep gouges in the sea floor, missing Merya by mere lengths. She bolted from her burrow for the safety of shore, slicing through the black, brackish water, hearts racing and gills spasming, scales still too thin and fragile in the icy currents.

Bare slivers of moonlight lit her way, jolting wildly in the churning shallows. She had nearly reached the protection of the rocks when a *boom* sounded through the bay, chased by a sharp, splintering *crack*. Her body, still attuned to the tunnel's hum, felt the break like it was one of her own bones.

She shot back toward the sea with speed she had not known for centuries, the crack still snapping down her spine. In the darkness and her desperation, she nearly collided with the tunnel. Merya reared back and began to sing, scouring along the slabs, listening for a break in the song they brought back to her. The currents buffeted, trying to drag her away, but she persisted.

She sang until the echo returned with a rift in its melody.

She tracked the tear to its source: a crevice in the concrete, trestles torn from their posts by a giant, tilting ship still tugging at its anchor, wedged beneath a beam.

Memories of the tunnel's voices and laughter and music rose through her. As water surged into the fissure, Merya's mind stretched further back, to calmer, clearer waters and fractured blue crab shells.

Her body coiled, resisting the gift she knew she must give—the gift she would always give to that which was broken in the bay.

The pain was sharp and searing as she tore the first scale away from tender skin beneath. Teeth locked tight together, she pressed her gift over the fracture, watched it meld and harden and heal, becoming one with the tunnel itself.

So Merya pulled the scales from her body, one by one, and gave them to the tunnel. Her spine twisted and thrashed with each wrenching tug, the raw line of flesh smarting in the scouring sea. And still, she pried away pieces of herself until the cement scar was perfectly sealed.

Her task complete, she released her writhing body from its work, letting the tides toss her limply to the sand. As awareness flickered, she burrowed back into the sea floor, sand and shell shards shredding fragile skin.

It would take many, many years to restore her sacrificed scales; these waters, once gentle and giving, were not the healing force they had once been.

But hope was a thing that endured, and so was she.

And so Merya slept.

# Mrs. Hensley's Home for Well-Behaved Spirits

## MERIT LA FRENIÈRE

*HARRISONBURG, VIRGINIA — 1953*

On the corner of South Main and a street that no longer exists, just past the Episcopalian church and the old dairy co-op, sat Mrs. Hensley's Home for Well-Behaved Spirits.

The sign was hand-painted and rather small. It was the sort of sign one only noticed if one had lost someone recently. Otherwise it blurred into the background, as such places are meant to do.

Widow Hensley ran the establishment with all the crisp efficiency of a retired librarian and the moral clarity of a disillusioned nun. She served tea at 3:00, locked the parlor windows at dusk ("open sashes invite mischief"), and insisted that no one wail louder than the radio during baseball season. She wore lilac talcum powder and had never once missed church, though she suspected the minister was an idiot.

The spirits?

Well, they minded their manners.

They came to her house by fog and funeral bell, by attic draft and door left ajar. A Civil War drummer boy who bled out in

Dayton. A grandmother who refused to die until her peach trees bore fruit. A postman struck by lightning on his second-to-last route. (He still tried to finish it. She gave him a small basket and let him hand out clippings to the pansies.)

They lingered, politely. No moaning, no clanking chains, no unsightly ectoplasm.

Harrisonburg, you see, had *standards*.

***

Then one spring morning, a knock came at the side door—the one used for milk deliveries and *special callers*. Mrs. Hensley opened it to find a man in a crumpled tweed coat, tie askew, hair like someone had broken an oath on his head.

"Are you the proprietress?" he asked. His voice had a city crackle to it. "I'm looking for someone."

Mrs. Hensley studied him. *Not a ghost.* He smelled too sharp. Like nicotine, worry, and the wrong kind of shoes.

"We're not accepting guests," she said.

"She used to live here. Years ago. Before she died. Her name was Claire. Claire Duprée."

Mrs. Hensley did not blink. "You'll want the Episcopalians for that sort of question. Or the Catholics, if you want flair."

"She wrote me letters," he said. "Until 1951."

Mrs. Hensley pressed her lips thin. That had been a particularly chatty year for Claire.

***

The man introduced himself as Arthur G. Penrose, out of Baltimore, and he insisted on paying for a room.

"Just one night," he said. "I won't cause trouble. I'll keep to myself."

Mrs. Hensley stared at him so long the air around them grew uncomfortable. Even the curtains in the parlor swayed backward. At last she said, "You may take the middle attic. It faces the cemetery. Kindly refrain from bleeding."

***

That night, the spirits were uneasy.

The postman hovered over the hall table, rearranging circulars no one had sent. The grandmother wept into a bread tin. The Civil War drummer boy stood watch outside Arthur's door, tapping a slow cadence with ghostly fingertips.

Claire, however, did not appear.

"I think she's hiding," Arthur whispered to no one in particular. "I just wanted to say goodbye. Properly. She deserved that."

Mrs. Hensley made him toast with apple butter and told him it was none of her concern.

***

At 3:17am, Claire arrived.

She wore her funeral dress, though the hem had mended itself. Her hair was gathered in soft 1940s curls, and she looked at Arthur with the weariness of a woman who'd *already forgiven him* once.

"You were supposed to come back," she said. "And I was supposed to be someone else by then."

He dropped to his knees as if the whole house had folded beneath him.

"I was afraid you'd moved on."

Claire glanced around. The linoleum rippled beneath her feet. The walls softened.

"I did," she said. "Just not as far as you think."

***

They talked until the crows called morning. She told him about the peaches. About Mrs. Hensley's porridge. About death being boring once you've alphabetized the other side.

He told her about the war he never fought in. About the book he'd never finished. About the woman he married to spite himself.

Claire kissed his temple and said, "That sounds like you."

He wept.

And then she was gone.

***

Mrs. Hensley found Arthur the next morning with packed bags and a ten-dollar bill on the mantle.

"I'll recommend your place," he said. "Discreetly."

"Don't," she replied.

He hesitated. "Did she seem...well? Happy?"

"She's dead, Mr. Penrose. But she's better than she was." Mrs. Hensley opened the door for him. "Some of us improve with distance."

***

That night, the ghosts were calm again. The postman rested. The drummer boy vanished altogether—perhaps finally discharged. Claire hummed in the laundry room.

Mrs. Hensley steeped her tea, turned off the porch light, and added Arthur's name to her little black book with the others:

*Arthur G. Penrose – Returned.*

*Alive. Unwise. Brief.*

*Left no forwarding address.*

She tapped the ink dry, closed the book, and smiled faintly.

"Well-behaved," she said. "More or less."

**POSTSCRIPT**

From a handwritten note slipped into a donated copy of *The Better Homes Manual of Tea-Time Etiquette* (1954), found at the Green Valley Book Sale:

*The key is in the birdbath.*
*Ask politely.*
*No shrieking after dusk.*
*If you see Claire, don't mention Baltimore.*
*—H.*

# They Called the Body Jane

## MEGAN MCCLINTOCK

THEY MEET AT THE corner of Boundary Street and Duke of Gloucester, as always. She's wearing a different body now—shorter, rounder, moles and eczema trailing up her neck. He looks exactly the same.

"You're wearing this one a bit thin, don't you think?" she says, looking him up and down. She holds out a paper cup. "For you."

He accepts the cup, breathes in the steam. "I'm afraid I've shown up empty-handed. Is it silver or gold for the four hundred and sixteenth anniversary?"

"That's all right," she replies. "You can bring the coffee next time."

She loops her arm through his and steers them down Williamsburg's cobblestone streets. They stroll through throngs of people—students, tourists, locals running with their dogs—toward the old Market Square. It's a while before he speaks again.

"I know I'm pushing it," he confesses. "I—I like this one's life. I like the wife. I like the kids. They're... nice."

She clicks her tongue. "That's why I go for single folk. No mess. No cleanup. No guilt."

He shakes his head. "I just want a little more time."

"It's started, though, hasn't it?" she asks, eyes trailing over the clothes hanging off his frame, the belt on his jeans looped through the tightest notch, the faint yellow undertone to his skin.

He hums noncommittally. "Have you been to Jamestown yet?"

She stops in the street. "Where did *that* come from?"

"I, you know." He shrugs. "I was only wondering. Since... well..."

"Since they found my bones," she replies.

He shrugs. Her jaw clenches. She pulls him to continue their walk.

"I didn't think they would ever find me," she admits. "Not really. Not...where I was."

"It was right outside the old church," he says. "Not so outside the realm of possibility."

"In the trash pit!" she snaps, her voice loud and sharp.

A family with two young children rushes by, the parents pointedly avoiding their general direction.

"They tossed me in the trash." Her voice cracks. "The archaeologists couldn't tell what was *me* at first. Did you read that, too? That I was all jumbled up with the dogs and horses?"

He lays a hand on her shoulder, and even though their bodies are new, the gesture is achingly familiar. "I'm sorry, Bess."

Bess looks away, wiping at her eyes. "They found knife marks all over me, you know. Like they were scraping me clean. Getting all the meat off the bone. I was fourteen. I was a *child*." She clears her throat. "And I can't even blame the others. Because after that first Jump, when I woke up in Mary's body, I was so goddamned *hungry*, all over again. It was hell. The confusion, the madness, the anger...You remember how it was, the first time. The horror of it all."

He grimaces. "God, that winter... I still have nightmares, sometimes. Not so much of the first Jump, though that was bad enough. I dream about the time before, when we couldn't find any more rats, and we started boiling our shoes—" his voice catches. "I can't stand the smell of leather. No matter what body I'm in, I get sick. Vomit right where I stand. Confused the hell out of Ally the first time..." he trails off, face tight with regret.

"Is that her name? Ally?"

He nods, twisting the simple gold wedding ring on his finger. "She didn't seem to mind when it happened. When I came in. I don't think it was a happy marriage, before." He frowns. "I keep thinking, maybe I could stay till the end, this time. Maybe that would be kinder than giving him back."

Bess shakes her head. "No. Two years. That's all you get."

"But—"

"*John*," she cuts him off. "No. It's too cruel, otherwise. You feel it, don't you? This body—it's fraying at the edges. Unraveling already." She rests her hand against his cheek. "Don't kill the body, John. Don't condemn his kind, loving family to a dead father. Give him back."

His jaw clenches. "I just—"

"No body can withstand the weight of a second soul," Bess says, a sad smile on her face. "Don't destroy this one to buy yourself another year."

They're in front of the Governor's Palace now, and John looks up at the tall brick building. "I remember it burning down, the first time. It was never the same, after."

She shrugs. "It's never the same, at first. But we get used to new bones soon enough. We always do." Bess pats his arm. "What if I let you take me down to Jamestown?"

John looks down at Bess, at this face he's never seen before and may never see again. It's beautiful, like all the others. It always is. "You would go visit your bones?"

She doesn't answer for a moment. Her eyes track the lines of tourists. "This place is like a palimpsest. I can almost see what it used to be, underneath." Bess tugs his arm, and together they walk back down Duke of Gloucester Street. "I haven't been back to Jamestown in a long time. I think it's become something mythical in my memory. If I can see it as it actually is—just dirt and brackish water, a vestigial place, frozen in time—maybe I can finally let it go."

They walk in silence till the end of the street, and the air feels lighter now.

"For what it's worth, people care about what happened to you. I wouldn't be surprised if they have an exhibit just for you," John says. "Made you the face of the Starving Time. 'See how bad it really was in Jamestown in 1609.' " He adds as an afterthought, "They called the body Jane, you know."

Bess pats his arm. "They can call it whatever they like. After all, it's not my body anymore."

# Run the Ridges

## DAVID HORN

THE FOG ALONG LOFT Mountain is thick enough to muffle my own footsteps. Dawn hasn't fully broken just yet; it's a pale smear behind the trees. I'm halfway up the ridgeline when I see him again; the same man along the trail ahead of me.

For the third morning in a row.

"Sir?" I call out. "You all right?"

He doesn't turn. Doesn't hesitate. Just walks like the ridge has somewhere it needs him to be and he's the only one on schedule.

The fog parts around him as if it remembers the shape of his body. I tell myself it's a morning illusion, nothing more.

I tell myself that every day.

My radio hisses. "Vega, trail cam flagged motion again at 06:17."

I check my watch. 06:17. I look up. He lifts his foot, sets it down in the exact rhythm I remember.

When the fog thins again, he's gone. There's no turn in the trail. No dip in elevation.

Nothing.

No mark the trail ahead. Only mine appear behind.

Back at the Loft Mountain shed, I pull up the trail-cam footage. At 06:17:04, the man walks into frame. His cap is pulled low, and his jacket is zipped to the throat. At 06:17:05, he has the same stride, same posture. At 06:17:06, identical. The background fog shifts, a branch trembles in the breeze, but he doesn't change at all.

I rewind to yesterday. Same timestamp. Same second, same man, same frame. I sync the videos, playing them side by side—two separate days, one perfect loop.

A photo tacked above the desk shows a group of CCC workers from the 1930s. One wears a similar cap. But that's not enough to explain any of this.

"Not possible," I whisper.

I jump ahead to 06:21. One moment he's walking. The next, he's just...not.

Then something else appears.

Me.

I watch myself stroll into the camera's view, stepping with the familiarity of someone who's walked that ridge a thousand times. My posture is easy, shoulders loose. At 06:21:42, the me on the screen pauses.

I don't remember pausing.

Frame by frame, she turns toward the camera. Her head tilts at an angle I've never seen myself make.

Then she smiles.

Small.

Like she knows something.

The real me feels a cold thread tightening down my spine.

I hike back up the ridge, needing proof the world hasn't gone sideways. Fog clings low and heavy. The trail is silent except for my breath and the far-off hum of Skyline Drive.

A figure forms in the white. The man. Walking his same impossible route.

Then another flickers a step behind him; same shape, but out of sync, like a corrupted copy.

"Okay," I breathe.

Movement to my left. I turn.

It's me.

Or it looks like me: same hat, same ponytail, same sure-footed rhythm. Twenty yards away, pacing the ridge like she belongs there more than I do.

Farther down, another version appears—my old uniform from years ago, hair shorter, back when I thought about leaving the park for good. Beyond her, a shadow shaped like me but with no hat at all, head bent as if listening for something deep in the soil.

None of them look at me. They walk with the same steady purpose as the man, like the ridge has a pattern and we're all part of it.

The closest one—my double today—pauses. The closest one—my double today—pauses. Slowly, she tilts her head down the trail. Not at me. At him. Then she steps forward and continues. Then she steps forward and continues.

My heartbeat stutters, then evens out to a rhythm that feels... mirrored.

This isn't haunting.

It isn't ghosts.

It's something older.

A pattern the mountain keeps. A pattern learned from boots and breath and repetition.

People disappear in Shenandoah more often than we talk about: lost hikers, old families forced out when the park was created, workers who broke their bodies carving these trails.

Maybe the mountain remembers them the same way it remembers wind routes or deer paths.

Maybe it's remembering me.

The fog curls around my boots like recognition.

I could turn back. I *should* call this in and pretend none of it touched me. But the ridge already knows my pace, my route, the exact moment I stop each morning to catch sight of the valley.

It has gathered enough of me to replay forever.

Another version of me appears ahead. Older, hair gray at the temples. She walks without fear, steady as the rising sun.

The ridge doesn't haunt the dead.

It keeps the living.

It runs them like weather patterns, like river flow, like seasons.

Wind stirs the fog, and for a moment I see all of us—every version—moving along the ridge in quiet synchrony.

Somewhere beyond the cloud cover, daylight is already burning through.

I take a breath and step forward, falling into rhythm with the pattern I taught the mountain.

My boots land where theirs did.

And the ridge runs the ridges again.

# Ghost Story

## KENT M. PETERSON

WE WERE HIGH SCHOOLERS whose parents had rented the Palladio at Barboursville for us to have a Halloween costume party. Some of us got bored around sunset and started milling about outside, playing tag and fake lightsaber fights down the parking lot, along the lane, and into the boxwoods on the hill opposite. Joel stopped at the sign warning it was trespassing after 5:30pm; I said, "Stop worrying!" and smacked Kyle with my cardboard sword. As the twilight deepened, we one by one wandered up to the hilltop with the old brick walls, with the plaque about Thomas Jefferson's architecture.

Charity and her little brother Simon were already there, circling the ruined house.

"It's spooky," someone said.

"The empty windows," Charity said. "Like skull eye sockets." Suddenly she glanced around. "Where's Simon?"

"Here," he called. "Door's open." The security gate into the cellars stood ajar. Too tempting; we filed in, wandering through the brick archways, the night sky high above us. We gradually gathered in the center of the big octagonal room, below the great hall before the floors burned with the house.

"We should tell ghost stories!" Charity said. "I'll start. One night a boy saw a skeleton outside. But nobody believed him. Every night the skeleton crept closer, but the little boy's parents told him to stop dreaming and pulled the shades tight. Then the skeleton broke in and pulled off his skin and wore it. And it still goes to school today!"

"That was a ghost story?" Justin snorted.

"Okay, you try, smarty-pants."

He thought for a minute. "Last Halloween, I was walking by the graveyard. The gate is only open for funerals. I heard a voice saying 'Stay.' I looked—there was no one there, but the gate was open."

"Ooh, nice. Okay, who's next?"

We were all silent for a few moments.

"I have wanted to tell this for a while," someone said in a low voice. In the darkness I couldn't tell who. Connor? Kyle? Maybe Joel. He liked doing radio-announcer impressions.

"I had been called to Fredericksburg to dispose of a late relative's estate, returning to Charlottesville in a buggy with trunks of papers and other items. I had in mind some alternate roads for the journey to make it swifter, but misled myself and lost my way.

"Arriving at a crossroads, I paused to determine my direction and was hailed by a young man—well-clad, but unshaven and uncombed, clutching to his chest a string-tied parcel wrapped in brown paper."

"Stop the old-timey talk already, it's tryhard," Charity said. But he continued in the same tone.

"He asked if I might take a passenger. When I said my destination was Charlottesville, he replied: 'It's all one to me. But I must be away from here, if you would be so kind.'

"I saw no reason to decline. We made good progress. My passenger assisted me with the itinerary, although considerably on edge as we proceeded, saying only that he would be relieved to arrive in town. We were near to country I knew well—on that very road below, just passing the abandoned farm—when a wheel slipped and broke several spokes. I keep some tools for just such an occasion and set to work. It was while I was thus engaged that we were approached by a woman.

"She was very beautiful—generously proportioned with amber locks down her back, though her face was streaked with tears. Upon seeing my passenger, her breath caught and she reached out, saying only 'Please.'

"He whirled and saw her. I have never seen a man so afraid, nor so furiously angry. 'You!' he shouted. 'I will not! I tell you I will not!' He jumped from the buggy and ran up the hill, still clutching his package. Her hands went to her face momentarily, then, weeping, she followed him.

"Discomfited at witnessing such a scene, I attended to the wheel. As I worked, I could hear voices from atop the hill, where this ruined house stood. Tense, angry, indistinct. After some time, they fell silent. By the time my repair was complete, the sun was setting, and I was feverish to be off, not wishing to stray in the dark. But I had agreed to a passenger, and I am a man of my word.

"I climbed the hill, as you did. I walked around the house, as you did. I found the cellars, as you did. All was still. I called out with no answer. In the lantern-light, I found a single bootprint. I entered and searched. In the great octagonal chamber, I found a scrap of brown wrapping paper and a bit of string, quite like my passenger's parcel. But no sign of any person.

"I turned to go, and saw him—the young man—high against the ruined walls, hanging from a cord wrapped about his neck, looped around the brickwork above. From his bulging eyes and the color of his face, he was clearly quite dead."

Complete silence for a few moments. I couldn't breathe, I was listening so hard.

Then Simon spoke up. "What happened to the woman?"

"Shush already," Charity said furiously. "Kevin's about to tell us and you're ruining it."

"Me?" I was startled into speech. "I'm not telling it, Joel is."

"What? No, I'm not," Joel said. "It was Kyle."

Kyle lit his lightsaber, gleaming on pale and tense faces. "I wasn't telling it," he said. "I thought Kim did her boy voice."

"Not me," Kim said definitively

"Whoever it was, stop joking around," Charity said impatiently

Nobody said anything.

"But what happened to the woman?" Simon repeated.

We stared at each other. Then a voice returned to us like a whisper on the wind.

"No one knows."

Silence again.

Then Charity spoke: "Anyone want some pumpkin pie?"

"Let's get going," Eric said.

We all rushed out together and ran down the path to the lights, the restaurant, and the people.

# Theophany on the Stockton

## MADELINE BARNICLE

WE HAVE BEEN ALMOST as transient as the humans, falling and rising, ready to surge onward. By their counting, it is the sixth day of the new year, although humans find a way to squabble about even this. Their cousins on the other side of the world dispute the reckoning of days and years, but they worship in the same rites. Here, at the place the humans call Stockton Creek, they have gathered to invoke a blessing upon us.

It charms us that they should see fit to petition the ever-flowing one on our behalf. We talk about *them*, too, and more than once a year. Often bemoaning their waste and neglect. Sometimes amused by the charming follies they construct. Their houses of learning—crude and cold, but always dreaming of something more. That they need not endlessly cycle their words, but hand down what they have received, and encourage their children to build greater still.

(Never have we asked the ever-flowing one to crush dragons among us or among the humans. This is a perennial misunderstanding. Dragons are reclusive, cryptic beings, even touchier than humans, but they are not enemies.)

The priest completes his blessing, lowers a sprig of herbs among us, then splashes us across his flock. As they rejoice, we race on, giddy with speed. We have swelled to great heights, this winter, and it propels us east. The humans bestow upon us new names as we journey; Mechums, Rivanna. We twist, tease, double back on ourselves. When we chide the humans for failing to make progress, as if a dam separates them from those who should be their sisters and brothers, they warn us that they are not only static things compelled by gravity, but also dispersing to every point of the compass, carving new channels with each step. So it is with us.

We narrow as we emerge from the place they call a reservoir. Only humans would devour us with such recklessness that they risk running dry. Only humans would have the foresight to design an edifice where we might abound in plenitude, on their children's behalf. And fill it with fish, that they torment for sport. Say what you will about humans, but they are never boring.

The mountains recede, and we enter a broad road where we have reigned in even grander majesty. Now our name is James. The humans here rejoice that they are not ruled by a king, boast that this little piece of land where we contort has given them so many not-kings, but still they call us by the name of a man who never stepped on our shores, whose words were carried here by oceangoing vessels.

Three hours have passed since we traded blessings with the humans west of here, and another congregation stands on our banks. Again, they thank the ever-flowing one for taking shape among them. Sometimes in exquisite complexity and brilliance, like an ice crystal; other times, scalding and uncontainable, like steam. Again, like their far-flung cousins, they confess their terror of dragons.

The dragons they imagine are fearsome, fire-making beasts whose wings carry them through the sky, across the world. Sometimes they appear with handsome faces, and sometimes they flee from snow. Again, this is slander; dragons are touchy and territorial, and would much rather frolic in a familiar snow den than harass humans several towns away. But it is not, altogether, inaccurate. The humans merely project their own shame onto the name of distant beasts, now that their fires have made us loom tall, and there is no snow.

In this place, Richmond, we once said to the humans: *hitherto shalt thou come, but no further.* Later, they carved an incision, claiming they did it on our behalf, to bind us together with our kin to the west. As if we were not already joined, in the endless dance of sun and gravity. It was the humans who sought unity, even as they held others in bondage.

But once a year, wherever they are, they pause to honor the ever-flowing one. And we who have been twice-blessed think it only fair to sing on their behalf. That someday they, too, may know the joy of being yoked together and forming something greater than themselves.

# Back of the Dragon

## KURT JOHNSON

FOR THE LAST FORTY years I've flown alongside my parents from continent to continent, igniting fires, terrifying people, and creating general mayhem, which is typical for our species: *Draco Gigantes*; loosely translated, "Giant Dragon". My parents embody a scorched-earth mentality, and I go along because they say that's what dragons do. But I'm pretty sure they don't think I'm particularly good at it, and I never seem to have as much fun as they do.

On the advice of one of my father's former clients, King Voltaire IV, we flew from Europe to North America in search of a secluded spot to brumate. Exhausted from our cross-continental escapades, we decided on Virginia. Dad had heard the King talk about this part of North America and the wonderful places to rest beneath the surface of the earth. The King called them caverns and said some spanned miles long.

Mom and Dad told me en route that it was time for me to find my own way, secure a mate, and continue our legacy. To emphasize their point, they abandoned me in southwest Virginia while they continued north to Luray. I expected this to happen eventually; it always does with *Draco Gigantes*.

I was alone for the first time in my life. I needed to find a mate, but how? I like lady dragons, I think, but I've only seen one in my life and it's my mom. They failed to mention where I would find a mate, but maybe this area of southwest Virginia would be flush with female dragons.

I soared in the sky to locate an acceptable brumate spot. My dragon sonar homed in on subterranean cavities created by a series of caverns between the towns of Marion and Tazewell. I dove hard into the earth near a town called Chilhowie and burrowed my way to Marion. My powerful wings and razor-sharp talons exploded through the softer layers of earth. Breathy flames incinerated the more challenging spaces. I created quite the disturbance along the way as the earth mounded over my size. Fully buried from snout to tail, I slowed, then stopped, nestled comfortably where I would spend the next half decade or so.

Brumating is like hibernating. The biggest difference is that reptilian creatures don't sleep the whole time we're brumating, like mammals do. Although I'm not always asleep, I do rest a great deal. When I am active, I nose around for water. Brumation isn't just one winter season for us. Ours can span years of cold seasons, offering an abundance of time to consider the important things in life.

Like now, I'm wondering what that racket is above me. I've been down here for five years, give or take, and I can't tolerate the noise much longer. The blasting, pounding, and vibrations are giving me one big backache. As I was about to burst through the earth to see what the hullabaloo was, the explosions and tremors stopped. I drifted back into my state of semi-consciousness and again began to think.

*Why do I feel remorse when I burn down villages? Why do my parents find such pleasure in terrifying people? And, yes, how will I find a mate?*

***

It's time. My internal clock signals my emergence from brumate. I press my legs down into the earth and push upward. Nothing but a little falling rock and soil. *What is going on?* I try again, I barely budge. I attempt to move toward the way I came in... blocked. I have only one way to go: forward. I fire my powerful dragon's breath and blow ferociously into the earth before me. I stop only when I hear a voice.

"Hey, watch it!" she calls out.

*She?*

"Hello," I respond, "Who's there?"

"Nice job, you big galoot. You singed my perfect eyebrows."

"A lady dragon? Right here in front of me?"

"Yes, I got here about three years ago. You having a little trouble getting out, hon?"

I tried to respond without sounding too desperate. "I am, but how do you know that? What did you see when you came in?"

"I entered north of Tazewell. It's a nice spot. I've been here before in this very cavern."

"Right, good to know," I said. "But what did you see? Why can't I get out?"

"Oh, yes, that. As I arrived, I noticed a road to my south, newly constructed on top of your back, I'm afraid. It seems quite popular for the human creatures riding their two-wheeled contraptions. The way you burrowed yourself created quite the twisty-turvy topography. The engineers made the road to your form. It'd be a shame for you to disturb it."

"You care?" I ask.

"Sure, don't you?"

"I... I... well, yes, I believe I do."

"Then you can't leave unless you fix the road. I'll help. If you promise to do that, then I'll stay with you forever. Deal?"

"How will I get out?" I ask.

"Just follow me as I back up. I've already created the path. Once we're out, we'll put the road back best we can by using our breath to reshape the asphalt."

"It's a deal," I say. "If only my parents could see me now, here with you and caring about people."

"They know," she said. "Who do you think told me you were here and that we'd be perfect for each other?"

# Mother of Presidents

## ADAM S. CROWE

*Beep... Beep... Beep!* The strapped-down cargo gently rocked side to side as the flatbed truck backed up slowly down the uneven Virginia dirt road.

The presidential specters of George Washington, Thomas Jefferson, James Madison, John Tyler, and Woodrow Wilson sat on a long, low limb of a nearby tree. James Monroe, Zachary Taylor, and William Henry Harrison perched together on a higher branch. The branches provided excellent viewing of a grass field filled with giant plaster heads carved into faces—their faces to be specific. The heads were aligned in three rows with one spot remaining in the front.

"Here I come!" A bewigged George Washington said gleefully.

"Get over yourself, George," Woodrow Wilson drawled.

The truck stopped and workers released the straps holding down the ten-ton bust lying on its side. The tines of a nearby forklift slid smoothly into a large hole in the top of the head.

"Why is there a hole in the top of my head?" Washington gasped.

"At least you didn't roll off the truck like Abe did," Zachary Taylor, the youngest ghost present, replied.

"I should've been in the front row," Thomas Jefferson intoned as he spun a feather quill between his fingers, "I *did* write the Declaration of Independence, after all."

"How come you always get more credit?" James Madison asked. "They do call *me* the Father of the Constitution!"

"I don't make the rules," Jefferson replied dismissively.

"I was even on the $5,000 bill!" James Madison snapped. "How many of you can say that? None. That's who!"

"And yet, Mr. Madison," John Tyler interrupted, "you're in the *back* row."

"Sick burn, Tyler," Washington said with a snap, causing his wig to tilt oddly.

"Sick... burn?" Jefferson asked.

"I still don't think they got my face right," Monroe moaned. "What do you think, Harrison?"

"The sheer magnitude of their size is so extravagantly excessive that it raises the obvious question," William Henry Harrison declaimed. "Who, in all of creation, would ever desire to behold another person's face enlarged to such an overwhelmingly grandiose scale?"

"What's... with... all... the... words, Harrison," Tyler snapped. "It reminds me of your inaugural address."

With the lift of a crane, workers spun the Washington bust upright..

"Refresh my memory, why are we here?" Wilson droned.

"As the largest state delegation of the Dead Presidents," Jefferson said. "We were asked to oversee the movement of the so-called Presidents' Heads."

"I suppose she truly is the Mother of Presidents," Monroe reflected.

"Who is?" Taylor grunted.

"Virginia, of course," Tyler snapped, "Keep up, my boy."

The workers gathered the discarded padding and steel rigging, hauling it back into the truck.

The eight ghosts watched as the truck bounced down the dirt road. They sat quietly for some time, which for a ghost can be difficult to measure as seconds are situations, minutes are moments, and hours can be histories.

"I thought our legacies would have amounted to more than these... heads." Wilson spat.

"These statues are of us!" James Madison thundered. "Their mere existence proves we did something right!"

"But there are holes in all of our heads," Monroe quipped. "We look awful."

"And they stand in the middle of nowhere," Tyler added, gesturing toward the sea of plaster heads.

"I would strongly encourage everyone," Harrison intoned, "to momentarily redirect the full capacity of your observational and interpretive faculties toward that point of interest yonder that is occupying our immediate vicinity."

"Again, with all the words!" Tyler chided. "Can't you just ask, 'hey, what's that'?"

"Look over there!" Taylor yelled.

Down the same road the flatbed had left earlier, a large bus labeled PRESIDENTS HEADS TOUR rolled to a stop, filling the open field with the hiss of airbrakes. A small group of people stepped off the bus.

"Oh, they're gathering by me!" George Washington gushed.

"Is that Thomas Jefferson?" A boy pointed to a nearby bust.

"Nope, that's Andrew Jackson," the tour guide said. "Jefferson's in the back row between Madison and Monroe."

"See, Madison?" Tyler drawled. "You aren't *alone* in the back row."

The tourists gathered into a rough semi-circle.

"Welcome to one of America's most unique attractions," the guide said with her hands raised. "These iconic sculptures represent every U.S. president from George Washington to George W. Bush."

"But that's not all the presidents," the boy asked, pointedly. "Where are the heads of Obama, Trump, Biden, and... *Trump?*"

The adults laughed.

"The Heads were saved before any of the newer presidents were ever added," the guide said solemnly.

"Is that why they are all alone and forgotten out here in this field?" the boy continued.

The guide knelt in front of the boy and looked him in the eye for several seconds. The eight presidential ghosts sat quietly in the nearby tree, watching and waiting.

"These Heads are alone," the tour guide said quietly, "but they aren't forgotten."

The boy watched, entranced by the words.

"The Heads represent the pioneers of this fine country," the guide said. "And the visionaries that brought new laws, education, and businesses to our great land and laid the foundations of a world changed by their vision and inspiration."

"Hear, hear!" several presidential specters echoed.

"But not all were good presidents," a woman in the group observed.

"No, not all," the guide said, gesturing toward the silent faces behind her. "But they were all willing to step up, take the reins, and do the best they could."

She guided the group through the tall grass, reciting presidential trivia as cicadas droned overhead, then ushered them back onto the waiting bus.

The eight specters sat in silence.

"Will they add more busts in the future?" Monroe asked.

Who among us can say?" Jefferson mused. "But history, by apprising us of the past, enables us to judge the future."

# The Reeds of Percival's Island

## ROBIN E. BATES

"It's different every day," I tell her. "This little island." I mean, some days I guess it's the same, but after storms it's different. The water can get up so high it almost covers the island and you can see from the bank on the Lynchburg side how it reshapes some of it. It washes away the tents and things that people build on it among the trees along the smaller paths branching off the main trail. When we crossed on the old trestle bridge first and looked upriver to the far corner, Annie saw the reeds all on the Lynchburg side.

The reeds come up when the water is low and people walk out on them. But you never know how deep or where the reeds stop and the current starts, so I told her that it's not a good idea to go out into them.

"Who is Percival?" Annie asks.

"I don't know. Maybe nobody knows." I figure somebody knows but I don't. I like the fancy old-sounding name for the island where everyone walks on the main paths but people wander the other paths, too. Annie and I cut left and climb down over roots that carved dirt into stairs. We follow each other over little paths and find tents and fishing wire strung up between trees, and circles of stones, and gray shells everywhere. I pick up a shell and put it in my pocket. Annie does, too. I turn to look out over the river on the Madison Heights side where the water rushes harder. When I cross back to look for Annie, she is out in the reeds.

I wring my hands and step a bit closer out to her. The squish of my sandal in the river water stops me, the reeds around my feet. So I back up again onto the dry dirt, roots under my heels. It can't be that deep with the water only up to her knees—just over, really, stopping around the edges of her skirt. She laughs and leans over to splash her hands in the river, brush the tops of the reeds lightly with her palms, looking around at the light glancing on the surface of the water. I back up another step further to safety, not taking my eyes off Annie, catching my heel on a root and stumbling several steps. The breeze from the river picks up, twisting her hair around her face, swirling strands around her neck.

She looks over at me, laughing. "Wish for what?"

"What?" I call back.

"Didn't you say something?"

"No, what? Come back! I really don't think it's safe in the reeds!"

She laughs again and faces the river, gazing downstream, reaching her arms out as though she would let the breeze or the current carry her away if she stepped out of the reeds into the stream. She is turning the little gray shell over and over in her hand and closing her eyes.

She can't see me sigh and roll my eyes as I turn to step over the roots. Two, three steps back up on to the bank, safe out of the reeds and onto shore. When I look back to the river, I see no one.

"Annie! Annie?"

There is no one on any side of me.

No one standing in the reeds, no one in the current, no one on the island behind me. I run down into the reeds, sandals slapping into the water, reeds brushing my ankles. River cold on my legs, then river cold on my fingertips. Water is soaking the edges of my shorts. I am brushing reeds out of the way to get to where she stood a few moments ago. No Annie. No one there. I stop and stand still where she was.

The water is all around me. The reeds hold me still. I am still.

I scan the water. I scan the shoreline. People are walking around in the park on the Lynchburg side, pushing strollers or walking in pairs and talking. Down on my left I hear people walking on the trestle bridge. But here in the river it's just me and the water and the reeds and the place where Annie stood a moment ago. I touch the little gray shell in my pocket.

My breathing slows as the breeze from the river brushes my cheek and lifts a strand of my hair, tickles the hairs on my arms, my neck.

"Annie," I whisper, when the breeze picks up and a lock of hair brushes my face, caressing my cheek.

*Wish*, I hear. *Wish*.

The reeds brush around my legs and I close my eyes.

# 2609 West Grace Street

## SARAH BENTON

THE TELEVISION FALSELY DEPICTS someone like me as hopelessly confused by modern slang. My century's imprisonment has kept my vocabulary current. I know, for example, the new renter has no interest in "dating" the man standing in my kitchen. She has "friend-zoned" him.

I watch them. He prepares drinks by the sink. She sits. Only after scraping a chair across my hardwood. I reach for her hair, to make her feel how my floor must. My hand falls through her head, and her gaze doesn't leave the streetlights beyond the bay window. Forever oblivious to my presence.

I wish I knew how to haunt. Another fallacy of television. I would scare away this latest tramp. Get this place empty. Condemned. Demolished. Maybe then I'd be free. A worthy cause for sacrificing my floors.

But I have no influence. And renters always come. Time hasn't withered the appeal of West Grace. It *has* decayed taste. The friend pours fluorescent juice into half-liquored glasses. A small vial slides from his sleeve into his palm. I think it's to sugar the rims until he dumps it all in one glass.

I don't trifle with renters' affairs, but the vein pulsing madly in his neck compels me to follow him to the table.

"What did you put in that?" I snap.

He hands her the glass.

"Stop!"

Jumping through him doesn't win his attention.

"Katie!" I think that's her name. "Don't drink that!"

She thanks him, ignorant of my pleas sent from farther than outer space.

I grab for her shoulders – to shake her into hearing me, knowing my limbs aren't even smoke to her. "KATIE, DON'T!"

She pauses, lowers the glass from her lips, and swirls a finger around the ice cubes. Her pearly nail polish turns red, stealing the color from her face.

"Get out right now or I'm calling the cops!"

***

"I was so comfortable around him... But then... I just got this feeling," says Katie into her phone.

She's been "FaceTiming" all day, rehashing last night.

I've rehashed too. I don't know if *I* caused that miraculous feeling. I've tried yelling at her today, but my voice can't break our distance again. If it even did before.

"Proof?" Katie scoffs. "The nail polish turns red from a roofie." Her face contorts the longer she pauses. "It's science, Meredith! I wouldn't make it up!"

She flings her phone across the couch.

***

I haven't seen Katie's friends in weeks. She mostly stays in now, moping from room to room like I did when I first realized I was trapped. This weekend will be different.

Her mom is visiting. Movie and museum tickets hang on the fridge. And I heard her making a reservation for Lost Letter. She's planned everything. I think she needs this.

Her phone buzzes, and she runs to it, scooping it up and sliding to the window. "There are still tons of parking spots out front," she says eagerly. Then her smile shatters. "What..." She swipes away a tear. "No. Yeah. It's fine. Another weekend."

Katie didn't cry much after the roofie. She didn't cry seeing those "posts" of her friends together without her. But she cries a lot now. Snot everywhere, hyperventilating.

I stand by her bed. My hand falls in and out of her shaking shoulder. "You're not alone," I whisper.

She snuggles harder into her pillow. Soon, she falls asleep.

***

She "googles" cats every night. She wants to know how to get one emotional support certified. Presumably, to circumvent her lease.

The owner banned pets years ago. The only good decision he's made for my house. Dogs destroy. Litter boxes reek.

I watch her scroll the SPCA website, falling in love over and over again.

Sighing, I hover my hand on her shoulder. "Get the cat."

***

"Belle! You know you're not supposed to be up there!" They've fought this battle since Belle was a kitten. Katie always lost, but seemed okay with it. I didn't need to intervene. Unlike when I preheated the oven or started the lasagna timer when she forgot. Things I'd never been able to do were easy when they were for her. Even encouraging her to host dinner with her "crush."

"I have my nail polish on," Katie says, ending her frenzy around the kitchen to hug Belle. "Not that Josh would ever... It'll be great."

I'd be watching to make sure.

***

Katie sleeps in the room I died in. One night, I just stayed asleep. The television taught me it was likely an "aneurysm." I think I'll have another, listening to her on the phone.

"It's time to leave this dump. No... I love the Museum District, but I've vacuumed too many of those fuzzy centipedes."

And I've sent as many down the drain.

My house is beautiful. Historic. She can't leave. Even with that new ring.

Katie turns off the light, casting me into darkness. I glide through the wall and blow out the candle she'd forgotten in the kitchen.

She needs me.

***

Not intervening while she packed was like trying not to breathe. At first, I disappeared boxes. Then bugs and cobwebs. I even made it the same temperature across every room. None of it made a difference. So I stopped intervening at all. I needed to save my strength.

Josh carries Belle's crate away. I lock the deadbolt behind him and join Katie in the empty kitchen. She stares out the window.

A hand on her shoulder and I can make her forget Josh. Make her regret leaving. I can find a feeling to make her stay.

She twirls around, taking in every inch of plaster, brick, and hardwood. Tears swell in her eyes. It'd been so long since I'd seen those.

"I'll miss you," she says.

I know she isn't speaking to me. She personifies everything.

I grab her shoulder. "I'll miss you too."

With a sniff, her tears end. I watch her drive away through the bay window.

# Luellen with the Emerald Shoes

Carol Parris Krauss

Luellen lived in a tidy ranch house on Pitchkettle Road, where the Great Dismal Swamp pressed against Suffolk's suburban hem. Her room appeared perfectly ordinary, with stuffed teddy bears arranged on a pale peach quilted bedspread and math homework neatly stacked on her desk. At the foot of her bed, emerald green Mary Janes caught the light with unusual brilliance, as if they'd absorbed something from the swamp darkness beyond her backyard.

Every evening at dusk, she would slip through the gate in the back fence and sneak down to the weathered dock jutting into the black water. Her parents strictly forbid her from being alone near the swamp. Bald cypresses rose like ancient sentinels around her, their knobby knees breaking the surface. Spanish moss hung in gray curtains from the tupelo gums. She'd sit cross-legged at the dock's edge, her shiny shoes catching the last light, and talk to the creatures—the pileated woodpeckers drumming overhead, the cottonmouths slithering, the chorus of frogs barking in the reeds. And she'd trail her fingers in the water, watching the ripples spread across that mirror-black surface. She never saw the Hollow Ones below. They were absence itself, hunger shaped like water, and each time her hand broke the surface, they fed.

By October, Luellen's mother noticed her daughter's collarbones stood out sharply.

"Sweetheart, you're barely touching your dinner," she said, worry creasing her forehead.

"I'm just not hungry, Mama."

By November, her father insisted on a doctor's appointment. Dr. Ramsey at the Children's Hospital ordered bloodwork. The complete metabolic panel, thyroid function, and celiac screening all came back normal.

"Let's do an endoscopy," Dr. Ramsey said, his pen tapping against the chart. "Rule out Crohn's disease, any malabsorption issues."

The scope revealed nothing. Her intestines were pink and healthy. December brought more specialists. An endocrinologist tested her cortisol and growth hormone levels. A gastroenterologist ordered a gastric emptying study and checked for H. pylori. A psychiatrist gently asked about her eating habits and body image.

"She's wasting away," her mother sobbed in Dr. Chen's office. "Seventeen pounds since summer. What's wrong with my baby?"

Dr. Chen shook her head. "Mrs. Barstow, I've been practicing for twenty years. I've never seen anything like this. Every test is normal. It's as if something is draining her, and we can't identify why."

By January, Luellen was skeletal, her emerald shoes enormous on feet thin as bird bones. She couldn't walk. The hospice nurse, Heidi, a kind woman with soft hands and sadder eyes, would sit with her for hours.

"Nurse Heidi," Luellen whispered one gray afternoon, her voice barely audible, "could you take me to the water? I want to see my friends one last time." Heidi looked at the girl's parents, who agreed through their tears.

The wheelchair rattled over the uneven ground. The cypresses seemed to lean in as they approached. The water lay still and black as oil.

"Right here is fine," Luellen said. "I can see them from here."

Heidi stepped back, giving her patient a moment of peace. Luellen gazed at the water, at the reflection of bare branches above. She tried to lift her hand—to wave, perhaps, or to touch the surface one final time—but she was too weak. That's when the water lurched. It rose in a dark column, sleek and glistening. The Hollow One had no face, but it had purpose. Tentacles unfurled like oil spreading across glass, tipped with hooks of bone. It slithered onto the dock with a sound like wet leather, moving with terrible patience.

"Luellen?" Heidi called, sensing something was wrong.

The thing was fast at the end. It enveloped her in an instant, pulling her down into its mass. There was no scream—Luellen had no breath left. Just a soft sigh, and then silence.

When Heidi reached the wheelchair, her hand flew to her mouth. The chair was empty except for those emerald green shoes, placed side by side neatly. And beneath them on the canvas seat was a dark, spreading wetness smelling of old swamps and older hungers.

The water below the dock remained perfectly, impossibly still.

# The Widow's Light: A Statement by Captain Barnacle, Cat of the Tower

## MERIT LA FRENIÈRE

***(Dictated, in spirit, to an acceptable typist)***

LET THE RECORD SHOW: I was never particularly fond of Thomas Hale, though I tolerated his lap when it happened to be the warmer option. He insisted on calling me "Barny," which I ignored, and sang sea shanties in a key not recognized by nature.

Still. His vanishing was inconvenient.

He was lost at sea when his vessel disappeared in a fierce nor'easter near the Virginia Capes and oblivion. No wreckage. No survivors. Just a crate of tinned peaches that floated back to port, glistening and intact, as if the sea had spared one witness.

That left me with his widow, Margaret. They said she went mad after that—and perhaps she did. *I* find Margaret to be a not-unpleasant presence—prone to weeping into my fur without consent—but having the reliable instincts of a creature who knows her duty.

She keeps the lamp lit. Even grief couldn't snuff that.

That, I respect.

We live at Cape Henry Light, a stone spindle of madness and gulls, perched precisely between the land of the living and whatever echoing nonsense lies beyond. A thin place. Fog-choked. Foolish. And full of Margaret, who keeps writing letters to a man eaten by the sea.

Every Friday, she walks to the surf, shoves one in, and says something poetic like, "Come home," or, "The world is emptier than your promises," or, "If this is one of your stupid pranks, Thomas, so help me I'll..." Then she looks at me, expecting agreement. I blink slowly and sit on her foot. This comforts her. She mistakes it for affection.

And yet: the sea returns the letters. In bottles. In shells. Once, in the mouth of a dead eel.

Even I was impressed.

***

I have always seen things Margaret cannot.

She believes the lighthouse is haunted.

She's wrong. It is residential.

We host the usual minor presences—fog spirits, drowned sailors, a regrettable specter who was once a tax assessor—but none particularly threatening. Just bored. A bit clammy. I ignore them unless they knock things off shelves. (My job.)

But one night, something *else* was drawn to the beacon's blue flame.

Something large. *Familiar.* Rising out of spindrift, high above the waves.

It pressed its hand to the lantern glass, just once. Margaret pressed hers back, sobbing like an amateur.

I watched from the stair. The scent—blowing through the old window slats—was salt and cedar and wet wool. Definitely Thomas. Just wetter.

I meowed once. He turned.

We regarded each other.

I blinked first. He never did learn manners.

***

From that night onward, Margaret stopped sleeping. She trimmed the wick hourly. Spoke aloud to the wind. Boiled tea for two. Poured some in a saucer for me. I declined.

(The gull drank it. Died dramatically. Returned two minutes later as a minor poltergeist. Now he haunts the weather vane and squawks Latin curses during thunderstorms. I like him.)

Margaret began wearing her nightgown all day, quoting ship logs to no one, and feeding our best smoked fish to whatever ghost she believed was courting her.

Reader, she was not wrong.

***

Then came the storm.

The tower howled. The sea rose. And Thomas—idiot that he is—returned fully, shaped from tide and grief, like a memory draped in flotsam and jetsam.

Margaret ran to the top. I followed at a dignified pace. She pressed her hand to the glass. He did the same. They murmured something human and soft—syllables only my feline ears could catch... 'I told you, Thomas. I never liked your mother's Sunday brooch.'

Then, he vanished. Mist. Gone.

Margaret collapsed against the rail and whispered, "He came home."

I curled against her side, licking my hindquarters.

He did, in his way.

They always come back—to cats, or lighthouses, or unfinished conversations.

***

Margaret never left the lighthouse again.

She wrote even fewer letters. Took to humming sea shanties in a marginally better key. Slept upright in a chair, as if expecting a knock. The flame never failed.

Sometimes it burns blue.

I still watch the stairs. When the fog rises just right, I see a man's shape pass through the door. I hear boots. I smell brine and aftershave.

I do not greet him. I simply sit where he used to sit. I watch him watch her.

And when she dies—as humans tend to do—I will wait in the window for her return. Because if a salt-drenched fool like Thomas can claw his way back from the undertow, I expect nothing less from Margaret.

She's stubborn.

She'll find a way.

Until then, I keep the tower.

Because someone must.

Because the light matters.

Because the gull is terrible at paperwork.

And because ghosts, for all their noise, make excellent company—once you've taught them to use coasters.

**—Captain Barnacle**
*First Feline Keeper of the Cape Henry Light, Occasionally Possessed, Always Prepared*

# The General's Gold

## JANE LIMPRECHT

"REENACTORS—THEY'RE EVERYWHERE IN VIRGINIA, aren't they?" I pointed up the slope to our right, through the trees, where the Virginia Railway Express tracks ran parallel to the woods and the trail we walked on. "Look at those two men on the far side of the rails."

"That's colonial garb, for sure." My daughter, Laurie, peered at the men who wore fitted jackets, knee-length britches, and stockings. "They're dressed like folks I'd see at The Cheese Shop when I was in college. Popping in on their lunch break from Colonial Williamsburg."

"Fairfax County's not exactly Williamsburg, but we have our share of history buffs." I approached the edge of the path to see better. "They have a shovel and a box or chest. Let's see what they're up to."

"Remember, reenactors love to gab." Laurie chuckled. "Make sure we have an exit strategy."

Dried leaves and twigs crackled and snapped under our feet as we pushed low branches aside. The cool autumn air smelled of rich soil and fresh water from Accotink Creek.

The taller of the two men unwrapped his neckerchief to wipe his dirty face. He exhaled loudly, then thrust the shovel into the ground so it stood straight up. At his feet, loose dirt surrounded a hole.

The other man hitched up his britches so he could kneel by a rusted, hinged chest about the size of a mini-fridge. He opened the chest and looked in. A grin spread over his face. Nearly toothless. His realistic makeup was impressive.

"Look here, Samuel," the kneeling man said. "I do believe we've found the general's gold."

Samuel stuffed his neckerchief into his pocket, then bent and thrust his hands into the chest. Something clanked when he scooped into it. He lifted his hands. Gold-colored coins fell through his fingers, glimmering in the pale afternoon sun.

"They surely do shine, don't they, Jonathan?" Samuel bit on a coin as if to make sure it was real.

Laurie raised an eyebrow. I put a finger to my lips. Do thieves dress up as reenactors in Northern Virginia? Luckily, the shadowy woods shielded us.

"General Edward Braddock, the fool," Jonathan said. "Burying the coins intended for our pay. Letting us soldiers go hungry to protect his precious gold."

"To be fair, the horses struggled in the mud, with all that weight," Samuel said. "There were many miles between Alexandria and Fort Duquesne. But we found the treasure, my friend." He bowed his head. "We found it with young Daniel's help."

Jonathan sat by the dirt pile. "Daniel, poor lad, perishing with the general and so many of our mates. People said he went out of his head, ranting about a glade where the full moon touched the crossing of two springs."

"We were the only two who listened to his tale," Samuel said.

I had held my breath without realizing it. Now I let it out, relaxing my shoulders. They really were reenactors, not criminals. I signaled to Laurie to step out of the woods.

She called to the men. "Are you acting out the story of British General Edward Braddock's gold? Seventeen-fifty-five?" To me, she added, "Virginia, Maryland, and Pennsylvania lay claim to the buried payroll, and it's never been found."

Neither man replied nor even acknowledged our presence. Too late, I remembered reenactors don't like to break character. I tried a different tack.

"Hullo, that's a fine-looking chest you've unearthed." I tried to sound like an eighteenth-century matron. "Can thee tell us about it?"

That didn't work either. Maybe our voices didn't carry. I didn't want to get any closer to the tracks. They curved out of view two hundred yards east of us, and the trees muffled any noises, making it hard to judge the distance of an oncoming train. Unsuspecting walkers had died on these tracks.

Samuel seemed to recognize the danger. He turned to look at the railway and then back to Jonathan, still sitting by the chest. But instead of suggesting that they move, Samuel said, "How strange that Daniel said naught about this stretch of metal rails and wooden slats. If these woods are common land where stock can roam, perhaps it's a barrier they won't cross."

I'm all for historical accuracy, but this was too much. The next westbound VRE could roar through any minute.

"Hey!" I shouted. "Please move away from the tracks. The commuter train will come through soon. It's so fast you won't have time to run."

Again, no response. An instant later, Laurie grabbed my jacket and jerked me back. "The train is coming!"

I tripped and stumbled as the Virginia Railway Express roared into view, its silver cars gleaming in the late afternoon light. The earth beneath me vibrated. My body did, too.

Any second now, the engineer would lay on the horn to warn the reenactors. I prayed they could scramble out of the way.

The train thundered past us, rumbling and clacking.

But the engineer didn't lay on the horn.

The VRE clattered westward until the last car disappeared around a bend.

Beckoning to Laurie to approach the tracks with me, I braced myself for what we might find on the other side.

Nothing.

No body parts, thankfully. No jacket or neckerchief. No shovel, chest, gold coins. Not even the dug-up dirt pile.

"Where did they go?" Laurie said. "How could they vanish so fast with that chest full of coins?"

"Vanish." The hair on my arms stood on end. "The engineer didn't blow the horn because he didn't see the men. There were no men to see."

"We saw them, didn't we?" Laurie said, her voice quavering.

"We saw someone," I whispered. "But I don't think they were reenactors."

# Manifest

## JEANNIE MARSCHALL

THEY SIT HERE IN this dismal hut, huddled around the fire in cassocks whose hems have grown cold and rancid with dirt, calling themselves warriors of God. A creature that might once have been a deer is roasting on a spit over the flames. Daylight is retreating. The little room is filled with the smell of smoke, charring meat, and seven men's shivering, hollow-ribbed craving. I want to escape the stench but the weather is far too bitter outside, the fire far too tempting despite my nausea. The thing over the flames *might* have been a deer. Its antlers are all wrong. It has claws. Its entails are bubbling in a pot with the last wrinkled turnips, just below the roast.

I told them not to venture into the forest, not to set their traps—all they'd catch would be trouble. 'No, no,' they insisted. 'We shall be protected. Our mission is just and holy, we shall be protected. The devils that walk these feral lands shall not harm us. We walk in the light and we shall be protected.' As if repeating it thrice like the charms they are not allowed to utter might make it true. As if night is not flooding the valley even now, drowning the hut where it stands, holey on sodden timber feet.

Anyone can be brave when the sun is up.

Cloak pulled tight, I huddle on my pallet in the corner, trapping pockets of stale air against my skin in a desperate bid for warmth. I only touch the walls with one shoulder, and yet the joint aches from the lick of icy winds that seep through the cracks in the boards. It is still better than lying on the floor ...or joining the men whose bodies crowd around the hearth, though they be blocking all its heat and leaving me with only shifting shadows. I do not want to be near them, nor the carcass. I look away from the clustered settlers and find my eyes drawn toward the entrance of our barely adequate shelter.

Lying by the gust-rattled door, dried blood splattered across the floorboards, the dead creature's hide has a glow to it still, and I can hear its song. So can the brothers. They pretend it is angels. Really, it is not.

"Take heart, friend," a half-muffled voice snaps me out of my thoughts. One of the brothers, cheeks bulging as he chews, proffers a cut of dark meat to me on the end of his knife. "Here, share in our blessings this day," he says, and it sounds obscene around the squelching chunk in his mouth.

Behind him, the others tear into the roast with the urgency of near-starvation. The sound of mumbled prayers snared around the cracking of cartilage nearly makes my guts heave.

It had all gone wrong as soon as they cut the first straight pine. They should have known better—even back home on the Continent, the old gods that keep watch over the land do not take kindly to axe blades wielded with impertinence. Paulians the world over talk pompously about their divine rights, but in the deep among the trees, there are magics that can heal your weary heart, powers that break rock and spirit if you cross them. I have seen what splits the endless waves of the sea, the wide, snaking, glowing bodies that dance with the ships—and I have seen the broken hulls of whalers. What I have yet to see is a Celestial objecting to any righteous anger of this Earth's entities. When these men hired me straight off a dreamer-pilgrims' ship to aid them in establishing their mission in summer, I should have left them the moment they hacked away the first branch in their path. They plunged inland, intent on salvation, trailing pain. Two days later, they picked up their tools and set up an altar to claim this place in the name of their divine. To this day, they have never bothered to appeal to that which dwells watching among the hills. Is it any wonder the Natives refused to trade with us?

Worse still, when fall came the forest itself denied us, chestnuts and berries withholding their bounty, resentful branches bare of anything we might have collected and preserved. I tried—despite the holy men's frequent admonitions and their talk of sin and dark, forbidden arts, I slipped out onto the hissing land with what little of Craft I have and pled for mercy, pled guilty and ignorant—one lost, queer soul, already too starved to leave. The land felt gentle then, surprised. Full of promise even as winter came. They might have heard me eventually, these ones whose names we have not been given. Meanwhile the brothers, desperate and full of stubborn pious confidence, went and killed and cooked what they claim was a deer.

The worst part is, it smells delicious. All curses do.

There in the hut on my lonely seat, I shake my head *No* even as my stomach cramps. The brother shrugs and withdraws his outstretched arm, stuffs the meat between his teeth. A dribble of juices escapes, and he wipes it back between his lips with dirty fingers. I clench my jaw, my lungs full of dead magic. My heart is thudding. Between me and the one Settler foothold teetering on this old, rolling-mountain land lie twenty miles of snow, and no hope of finding my way to a Native settlement either.

When the bones are picked almost clean and the scratching of claws on the rickety door comes at last, I let the warriors of god draw their long knives and holy symbols, let them break out in loud claims of untouchability above the din outside, and close my eyes in mute acceptance. When the door splinters open, I uncurl my empty hands and offer up all I have left.

# An Encounter in the Great Dismal Swamp

## Arlen Fain

Not all ghosts are what we leave behind when we die. Real ghosts are what we leave behind as we live on. These ghosts are burning shadows of our former selves that may haunt us until we die.

***

David was lost. Which was impossible. Acres of this patch of swamp had burned clear. He should see open stretches of marshland. Instead, a thicket that wasn't supposed to be surrounded him. With no sign of pathways out. He sloshed through mid-shin-deep water. Also, impossible. When Jan and he had shored the kayak earlier, the area was bog but not flooded. And with darkness encroaching on the previously blue sky, he froze, unable to move as the drenched environs sludged in around him. Everything was a haze. Only the distant voices of what sounded like campers. Again, impossible. Camping was only in designated areas, far on the other side of the lake.

He looked for the others, but everywhere he was met with the entangled brush of an ancient woodland.

***

Jan tried to shake her grad assistant out of his trance. Nothing elicited any response. He was a statue—catatonic yet standing on his feet. Just the way she found him. How they had gotten separated was beyond her.

An hour into their investigation, they uncovered signs of a long-abandoned encampment and began collecting the aged artifacts they discovered: fragments of stone tools, clay pipes, the rotted remains of cabins. Immediately, David ran out of storage bags. The spare box was in the kayak. After sending him to retrieve them, she continued her walk, head down, eyes open. Searching. A while passed before she realized David had not returned and decided to backtrack. When he finally came into view, he was gone.

A hollow shell.

She took his arm and began leading him toward the kayak.

***

He snatched the container of polyethylene baggies from the boat. What a rookie mistake. It wouldn't surprise him if his professor fired him as soon as they returned to Old Dominion. This was a major find; he couldn't botch this up. He needed the assistantship and the experience.

Without another thought, he dashed back as fast as the soggy earth and random knee roots would allow. Halfway, he came to a halt. In his way stood a fiery pillar. It looked organic. Alive. Avian-like.

Its flames flickered like beating bird wings, its true shape never clearing. David noted the swamp had fallen silent. No frogs, no insects, no birds.

From the quiet, the forgotten sagas of the forsaken swamp slithered out of slave-dug trenches. Secrets hung suspended like spectral serpents from nearby cypress branches.

***

Drummond's surface was glass. The researchers rippled across the calm, passing ancient cypress, gliding on a springtime breeze. Within moments, they reached the intended spot. Pulling the kayak onto the boggy shore, Jan picked up an old board that looked weathered by centuries, with the ghost of the word *nansemond* painted on it. She knew this area had been Nansemond from colonial times until 1972, when it briefly became an independent city. But this was no marker she'd ever seen. Though preserved, it was brittle and rotten with age.

Jan handed the time-worn plank to David, who examined the board with his habitual gentle curiosity, turning it over in his hands, interrogating its texture.

"Should we collect it?" he asked.

"Probably not authentic." Still, it struck her as odd.

Her assistant only shrugged. "Not particularly. I mean, someone could've put it up here years ago as a memorial of some sort. Maybe it washed up after the storms. Like the site we're here to study."

"Maybe." She smiled. "Let's see what else we find."

David tossed the old slat down, making a soft splatter in the wetland mire.

***

Oars sloshed against the surface, slicing through green algae mats and duckweed. Dr. Jan Kerst lolled along with the sounding swirl, a sporadic thud of their handles drumming against the kayak's side. Her grad assistant, David, studied the root-covered banks of the canal, his gray eyes ferreting through the leaf cover and low-hanging branches for the opening to the ditch.

They were here to investigate evidence of a heretofore undiscovered maroon settlement, and Jan decided the best approach was to follow the canal. Her other option was on foot in using the series of hiking and hunting trails. They could have accessed these via park service roads. But taking the canal down to the feeder ditch and over to Lake Drummond would allow them to paddle by some sites she'd hoped to revisit—places previously studied. Doing so on this grant's dime made sense. They could easily traverse Drummond's cornea-shaped body to the burn scar between the Riddick and Interior Ditches. There, she expected to find artifacts believed to have belonged to a people who had escaped from enslavement and found refuge in the swamp.

Jan reflected on how much the words *escaped* and *enslaved* seemed, in her mind, to echo one another, creating a doubling effect. As though these terms somehow rhymed or were harmonious. Of course, her rational mind knew otherwise.

Jan felt the swamp doubled itself in another way, serving as its own antonym. *Great* and *dismal*. Though it was neither great nor dismal—not nearly as considerable now as it once was in its original state, and not nearly as dismal as other swamps and marshes she had studied.

Because the canal took longer, it meant their return would be around sunset, an even more stunning scene of the swamp. And speaking of stunning, it also meant more time with David. Her job was mentoring him in applied archaeology, but it didn't mean he wasn't easy on the eyes, in her scientific opinion.

When she looked at him, she saw so much promise. She also saw in the young man something more than talent and beauty—she saw a descendant of someone who had been a marooned resident of this very swamp.

# In Bad Faith

## Megan McClintock

THE MAN BANGS HIS fist on the dingy bathroom door at the Vienna Metro stop. "I swear to God if you don't let me in..."

"Now, now," a voice calls from inside. "No need to bring Him into this."

The door cracks open to reveal a woman standing in front of the mirror, adjusting her suit jacket. She's average-looking. Dark eyes, unkempt hair—the type to disappear in a crowd.

He frowns, steps forward. "I was here yesterday."

Her eyes lift to meet his through the mirror. "And?"

"No one answered."

Her lips quirk into a smirk. "You didn't follow the rules."

"I—"

"You took an Uber Black to the Metro stop yesterday. The contract is clear. To make an appointment, you have to ride the Metro from D.C." She turns and points to the toilet. "Take a seat."

He scoffs. "Are you serious?"

She leans against the sink and waits.

"That's disgusting."

The woman shrugs. He realizes she hasn't blinked this whole time.

He glances back at the toilet, lip curling up in disgust.

"Sit," she commands, like he's a dog. He pictures himself back-handing her across the face as he winces, crosses to sit on the Metro toilet seat. He thinks of the particles of piss and excrement on the toilet seat transferring to his custom suit pants, and his hand curls into a fist.

"So," she drawls. "Senator Eric Sadler. Why are you here?"

He leans forward. "I want to renegotiate my contract."

"Our contracts are final."

"I have a proposal that would be incredibly beneficial for your... organization."

She sighs and twists her hand. A silver dagger appears in her palm, smoke curling up from the blade, and she holds it out to him. "Remind me of the terms of your contract."

Sadler takes the handle and pushes the blade against his fingertip till blood wells and drips onto the knife.

She accepts the knife, brings it up to her mouth and stares into his eyes as she licks the blood from the metal. She doesn't look human at all now—more like an outline of a person, with something darker, sharper lurking underneath.

When she speaks, her voice is deeper. Her eyes flash red. "Twenty years of power. Influence. Wealth. A painless death." She shrugs. "A standard soul contract. And you've still got three years left."

He stands, takes a step forward. "Exactly. I need more time. There are major developments underway. Things that would benefit you even more than me. The party is floating me for the presidential primary, you see. Think of the power, the influence you could have! And of course, I could help you more directly. Funnel souls to you, help facilitate contracts. I was thinking of very modest terms—two additional years for every soul I bring you."

"You want to create a pyramid scheme for making deals with the Devil?" she deadpanned.

"Well, I wouldn't phrase it that way. But it would be a win-win for everyone involved. You get more souls, I get more time, we both get what we want. It's just good business."

She chuckles. "You think no one has proposed this deal before? You would be surprised how many bankers and multi-level marketers end up in Hell. Or, perhaps, you wouldn't be surprised at all. Either way, I'm afraid I have to decline your request."

Sadler stills. "Please." He clenches his jaw. "I just... I need more *time*."

She scoffs and turns her back on him to look at herself once more in the mirror. "The answer is no." She points the blade at the door. "You can go, now."

The world contracts. White noise fills his mind. He shakes his head, slowly at first, then faster. "No. No! I, I did everything I was supposed to do. I came *here*. I rode the goddamn Metro. You have to *listen to me*, goddammit."

Her eyes glow red. "What did I say about bringing Him into this?"

He stalks forward. "You're *going* to help me." He reaches out to grab her. To do... something. Something to make her listen. But his hand passes through her like fog.

The Senator stares down at his hand, and she reaches behind him with her other arm. She slams his head down into the sink like he weighs nothing at all.

There's a sickening crunch. Pain, so much pain, then nothing. Just pressure, and a strange ringing sound. The Senator collapses on the ground. Blood blooms across his vision.

The woman crouches next to him, and her smile doesn't reach her eyes. The lights in the bathroom flicker as she lifts a finger under his chin.

He slaps her hand away from his face, but it's weak. The world is fading out of focus, drenched in shades of red.

"I've still got three years," he wheezes. "Help me."

She shakes her head. "Sorry, Senator. You've triggered section 14c of your contract."

Sadler shakes his head, eyes glassy. "I don't... what do you...?"

"The Bad Faith clause. You were going to, what—throw my head against the wall? Choke me? Hit me? You thought of it. Not that I care what you think. But then you had to go and be so damned predictable. You, *Senator*, operated in bad faith. So, no. I don't have to heal you, or save you, or take away your pain, or do anything at all where you're concerned."

She watches him as the light fades from his eyes. The outline of her humanity falls away, and he sees her now. Sees her for what she truly is.

And it's not the blood loss or the brain damage that kills him in the end.

It's the fear.

His body tenses, slackens, dissolves into dust, custom suit and all.

***

The woman crouches down and sighs, running a finger through the pile of dust where Senator Eric Sadler used to be. "And they call us the monsters."

# Listen to Miss Nellie

## CAROL STEELE

"YOU SHOULD LISTEN TO me, Sheriff, there's something out there—"

"Miss Nellie, this is the third night you've phoned grumbling about something in the woods." Clark County Sheriff Frank Canton sighed and rubbed his left temple. "It's the woods. There's always something out there."

Nellie rolled her eyes and drained her glass of Canadian Club. "Listen you knucklehead, I've been living on the foothills of the Blue Ridge all my life, and I feel it in every one of my eighty-three-year-old bones. There's something big and bad out there. I sense it."

"Miss Nellie, you go to bed and everything will look better in the morning." He disconnected.

Nellie slipped her phone into her apron and shuffled to the gun cabinet. She loaded her Remington 12-gauge knowing that if she fired, more damage might be done to her bird-like frame than to any target.

Seated on a hard-backed rocking chair, she placed the shotgun across her bony thighs and pushed sheer white curtains from the only front window in the one-room cabin. A waxing moon lit the treetops that stepped down to the Shenandoah River as the water sparkled and gently moved northward, its sound barely audible in the night.

*Let 'em come.*

***

Morning light and stiff arthritic joints awakened Miss Nellie. She surveyed her bolt-hole, relieved herself in the attached lean-to washroom, and changed into a fresh cotton dress. After her usual breakfast of black coffee, fried eggs, and Gore bacon, she scrutinized the brush-free six hundred square foot area surrounding her cabin. She turned the last corner and came across the remains of a fox, coarsely mangled and recognizable only by one intact ear. Paws six inches wide left claw-drag marks about one foot long as the killer scratched through dirt, pulling turf onto the fox's remains in an attempt to hide it. Nellie scanned the dense forest and noticed two paths freshly cut. Both had tree branches broken ten feet up, on one path the debris faced away from the cabin; the other, the debris lay toward it.

With her shotgun in hand for protection and hope in her soul she'd identify the animal, Miss Nellie investigated both paths looking for signs of fur or footprints or scat. Or? What she discovered: Nothing.

***

Shortly after nine o'clock, a rusty Ford Explorer snaked up the single lane mountain road to the cabin and into view of Miss Nellie as she slowly propelled herself on her homemade birch porch swing. The driver, a young woman, waved with the enthusiasm of a want-to-be-chosen game show contestant. Once parked, the driver clumsily hoisted an open box of groceries onto the porch and placed it at Miss Nellie's feet.

"Thank you, Lucy, I do appreciate all you do. Sit yourself down and talk with me."

"Can't stay long, Miss Nellie, I've got to be out there hustling. You know, no deliveries, no money." Lucy slid her red hair from her scrunchie and re-secured her mane in a hocus-pocus maneuver that produced a sleek bun on the top of her head. "Tell me, why do you have your shotgun out here? Some critter getting into your compost heap?"

"I wish it was a nuisance animal. It's something bigger. Something worse." Miss Nellie dropped her head toward her chest and moved it side to side, intense worry emanating from the gesture. "I've been hearing animal moaning in the distance at night. And growling and"—she slapped her hands together with such rapidity and force that Lucy pulled back—"screams. In the dead of night."

Lucy looked at the half gallon bottle of whiskey poking from the box she delivered.

Miss Nellie kicked the box. "Don't be thinking I'm all liquored up. And you should listen to me. Just like I've been telling that no good sheriff, there's something out there. Last night it shredded a fox, absolutely tore it to pieces. Just around the corner there." She indicated over her shoulder to her left. "I used to think foxes were the most awful critters, killing just for pleasure, but no, there's a beast out there..."

Standing, Lucy leaned over and kissed Miss Nellie on her cheek. "Stay inside. Keep your door locked and your shotgun nearby. I'll expect your delivery order in two days but give me a shout if you want anything before then." Lucy forced a smile and sidled to her SUV.

***

As dusk fell, Miss Nellie sat on her porch sniffing the air. She cocked her head and shoved an ear forward as if seeking a strong frequency. Her faded blue eyes scanned the ground and to the top of every tree. Nothing. Absolutely nothing. Realization hit her; she couldn't remember the last time she saw a squirrel or heard a bird.

All silent.

Too silent.

***

Repeated midnight thunks of a large object against the outside cabin walls jolted Miss Nellie from a light doze. She eased from her single bed, grabbed her gun, and skittered to the front window as moonlight illuminated an enormous mass of animal flesh bounding into the woods.

***

"Miss Nellie, stop phoning me every night. There's nothing out there." Sheriff Canton's voice rose with his anger. "But I'll come up now and take a look. And when I don't find a darn thing, you've got to promise me you'll stop phoning."

"Thank you, Sheriff. Be careful."

***

Miss Nellie stood at her front window and stared down the mountain toward Route 7. Fifteen minutes into her vigil, a speeding Sheriff's car began to cross the Harry F. Byrd Bridge over the Shenandoah River. An enormous creature rushed head-on toward the car blocking any forward progress. It snatched the vehicle, twisted it into a gnarled jumble of metal, and heaved it into the water below, its lights still flashing. Within seconds, the animal lumbered from the bridge and vanished into the woods.

*You should listen to me.*

# The Trees

## CAITLYN BROOKE

ARLINGTON IS A CITY of transplants. Year after year, thousands of prospective residents flock to the county with lucrative job offers, searching for a higher quality of life (or just a better commute). No matter who they were before or where they came from, they all have one thing in common: they need a place to live.

Despite the demand for new housing and construction, the majority of Arlington's urban development remains clustered around a handful of Metro stations—dense high-rises in Rosslyn towering over rows of tiny, single-family homes that sprawl across much of the county's paltry twenty-six square miles. When I first arrived, I presumed this strange, uneven skyline to be the result of restrictive zoning, the likes of which haunt many major U.S. metro areas.

I was wrong. The housing crisis in Arlington has nothing to do with policy or urban planning, and everything to do with the Trees.

The loudest voices you will find at any given county meeting are the Arlington Tree Defense League (or ATDL, for short), a collective of home-owning, longtime residents dedicated solely to the preservation of trees. A sympathetic goal, to be sure—except when it conflicts with common sense. A tree grows into the sidewalk and tears up the pavement? Well, the tree was there first. A tree is about to fall on a power line, risking power outages and forest fires? It was a mistake to run a power line so close to where a tree might grow. Redeveloping a property with even a single tree within its borders? Out of the question.

*These transplants*, a woman from the ATDL hisses to her compatriots, *they don't respect the Trees. They don't understand what it's like, living next to the Trees.*

When she steps up to the podium, she wrings her hands, sweat beading on her forehead. The ATDL objects to the most recent study the county performed on Arlington's tree canopy. It states that the tree canopy has increased. This is wrong, she insists. That cannot possibly be the case.

"The analysis supports the conclusion that the tree canopy has indeed improved from prior years," the chairman of the board assures her.

She simply shakes her head. *It's not possible*, she insists, repeating it over and over for the full two minutes of her allotted time. Not once does she explain why she believes this so ardently.

With the beep of the timer, she steps aside and I take to the podium next. I'm here to speak in support of a new development planned for a vacant lot next to my apartment. A single tree on the lot must come down, but the developer's plans include new green spaces. The net tree count in the area will rise—an easy win for density and the environment.

The board agrees with me and likely would have signed off on the proposal even without my support. Still, for a moment, I feel a rush—like I've done something meaningful to make the world a better place. As I step down from the podium, however, I notice the woman from the ATDL shaking her head again.

*You do not understand*, she mutters.

Maybe I don't understand. But the part of me that can sense a gaze boring into the back of my head, or spot the shape of a predator shifting in the shadows, recognizes the trees that lie deep within the low-density neighborhoods of Arlington are not like the trees that line the streets of the Ballston-Rosslyn corridor. Those trees do not wave to people as they walk by with their morning coffee. Those trees are angry.

As I walk home, I avoid the quiet, unlit side streets. I avoid the Trees, their overgrown branches looming over the sidewalks, leaves like rows of jagged teeth waiting to snap shut. They do not chase me. The Trees have lived here for decades; they can stand to wait a moment longer for me to let my guard down.

*You are fighting a losing battle*, I want to tell them. *The new trees do not think the way that you do.*

I imagine their response: *They will, someday.*

When I am in the comfort of my small apartment, I draw back the curtains and step out onto my balcony. I glance over at the adjacent vacant lot. The single tree whose life I condemned glances back, leaves rustling in discontent.

*We have roots here*, they whisper. *Do you?*

# Lights in the Lake

## STEVE PORTER

A GOLDEN GLOW CAST over the rippling water of the lake, a light breeze cooling the summer air. Callie Bennett sat on the edge of the deck, legs hanging over the side. A slight lift of her head brought the Smith Mountains into view from across the miles of Smith Mountain Lake. Her mom always called the lake *the jewel of the Blue Ridge.* This was mom's happy place, once upon a time.

It had been too long since Callie visited her family's property on the lake in the heart of Virginia. The memories born here have stayed with her for the last fifteen years. Whether she wanted them to or not.

For fifteen years, she dreamt of the lake. Not every night, but often enough that it stuck with her. Callie never remembered her other dreams, but this was so vivid and frequent, that she could never shake it.

***

Quiet and serene, only the light from the moon shining against the water. She drifted out on the water in a kayak, lightly bobbing with the ripples; no paddles, the gentle pull of the current carried her to the center. When the moon fell behind clouds, another presence unveiled itself with a green glow from beneath the surface.

She tilted her gaze over the kayak's edge: dim, green lights shimmering in the depths of the lake. Dread and fascination warred inside her. Her dream always ended the same way; she leaned over the side of the kayak, drawn to the lights. She shifted her weight to the bow, until the kayak capsized and Callie fell into the cold water, jolting her awake.

***

Callie tried to go on with her life, to focus on anything other than that damn lake. She moved away, focused on school to push forward with her life. Just when she thought she moved past it, the dream came again. She fixated on it, to the point where it was the only thing she could think about. She bordered on obsession—her school and social lives taking a downward spiral. Callie knew that only one thing could help her overcome this nightmare.

She returned to the lake, to her family' s property, to settle with the nightmares that plagued her. As the sun fell beneath the mountain range, that same sense of dread began to swell. The last ray of light disappeared, and the atmosphere assumed an eerie chill. Callie watched the moon with intensity as clouds blotted out its light. Her breath hitched, and a deathly silence fell over the lake. She waited a few seconds for something, *anything* to happen, and...

Nothing happened. A pang of disappointment ran through her as she stood up. As she turned to head back to the house, she caught it out of the corner of her eye. A gentle glow beneath the surface. A rush overtook her, and she grabbed a kayak, launching out onto the water and hopping in. Ensuring she had paddles this time, she rowed out onto the water following the glow. Before she knew it, Callie found herself at the lake center—just as in the dream.

The faint lights intensified with rhythmic pulsing, like a beating heart. They illuminated the lakebed down into the depths. The pulsing light once again drew her in. She leaned over the edge of the kayak to get closer. The kayak lurched and flipped. Cold water slammed into her as she plunged beneath the surface.

Down, down, down she sank, an unseen force dragging her under. She fought to return to the surface, her efforts in vain as the pull only grew stronger. The green, murky water blinded her as she sank, the pressure gripping her lungs. She thrashed around in a panic, trying in vain to work her way up to the surface. Eventually, her energy faltered and she just sank, the last of her breath fading.

Then something strange happened: the murky water began to clear up and Callie could see the entire lakebed floor.

Buildings, farmhouses, and barns. All dilapidated and drowned, but all still standing at the bottom of the lake. An entire town drowned in the shadow of the mountain when the lake was formed. As she sank closer to the bottom, a haunting revelation imposed on her.

Ghostly figures walked the bottom of the lake, casting that green glow. Hundreds roaming along the bleak floor. Some tended to the sunken farmland, holding onto the vestiges of a past life. Others wandered aimlessly with no intentions. This wasn' t some flooded town or lost monument. The mystery at the bottom of Smith Mountain Lake was a necropolis.

She started thrashing her arms and legs again in a desperate attempt to return to the surface. Finally, she felt herself start to rise. Several of the ghosts turned their withered gazes at her. They rose too, effortlessly defying the weight and pressure of the water. The cold, decayed hands of a ghost wrapped around her ankle, stopping her ascent.

She whipped her head around, meeting the cold, dead gaze of the ghost. She froze and stared at the ghost, taking in the shock of its decayed visage. The grip of the ghost held firm, and its silent stare spoke a thousand words. In this silent exchange, Callie understood everything now. Why she had been plagued by dreams for all those years. Why she felt the yearning call to return to the lake.

It was them. The spirits of the lake—calling, beckoning to her across fifteen years. They still wanted her now, to take a place among the drowned congregation. As her final breath slipped from her lips and floated up towards the unreachable surface, she swelled with clarity. She was always meant to come home. Another spirit.

Another light in the lake.

# Late for Muster

## R.A.T. DUBRUELER

DANIELLE GRABBED HER SLEEPING bag from the passenger seat, double-checked the essentials in her backpack: water bottle, granola bar, hand sanitizer. She didn't need the bug spray. It had gotten too cold for insects in November, so she left the bottle in the car.

With the frost beginning to silver the ground, she carried her supplies into the clearing. The park had emptied with the setting sun, and Danielle savored the stillness as she set up her tent. Somewhere a fox barked, and her breath poured out in white puffs as she worked.

Cold Harbor Battlefield, a patch of land tucked behind a snaking, single-lane road in Mechanicsville, Virginia, was quiet now, its fields softened by grass and time. Danielle loved history; she'd spent hours reading about this hallowed ground, where a disastrous Union defeat during the American Civil War claimed twenty-thousand casualties between the two armies. During the bloody two-week battle, the dead outnumbered the living for days.

Then came footsteps. She stopped moving, and her ears perked, listening for the random crunch of an animal. But the steps continued. Slow. Deliberate. Danielle stiffened, trying to gauge the direction. She pointed her flashlight toward the noise, its beam cutting across the countryside, but she saw no one.

She reached for the pocketknife in her backpack, her heartbeat picking up speed, when she felt a tap on her shoulder. She turned, her numb fingers failing to grip the knife's handle, and she gasped as she shone her light into a man's eyes.

"Sorry to startle you, ma'am," the man said. "But you're late."

Danielle's mind scrambled for words. "I—I'm sorry," she stammered. "Who are you?"

"You're late," he repeated. "And we can't keep them waiting."

Danielle looked around. They were alone. "Late for what?" she asked. "There's no one else here."

"The muster. We have to go now." Then, he turned and began walking toward the tree line, a slight limp to his left leg.

Was this a prank? A ghost tour? Danielle could've gotten in her car and driven home, but curiosity forced her to follow. As she neared the copse of loblolly pines, figures emerged in the flashlight beam: a row of men in blue and gray uniforms, impossibly still.

Danielle crept closer, unable to look away. The man who had summoned her stood separate from the rest as he announced slowly, methodically, "Cooper. Davis. Williams. Carter."

As he called each name, a man from the line stepped forward. Danielle remained frozen, not from the cold but in sheer astonishment. What was this? A reenactment?

The man who had found her stood inches away, and he was covered in blood.

"Answer the roll," he said.

As she turned to run, she tripped over a broken branch and fell hard, her flashlight skittering across the frozen soil. She sucked in the cold air, and as she did, the scent of gunpowder filled her throat. The temperature dropped.

"Anyone who deserts their comrades is to be put to death!" the man—no, the soldier—thundered above her. "It's the only way the line holds. You refuse your duty, you face the penalty!"

"I'm not deserting anyone!" Danielle cried, finding the strength to stand and run. Quickly, mist gathered, crawling over her lips and into her lungs, thick as a shroud, and after a handful of strides, she plunged into a winding trench. She landed with a thud, heard her ankle snap before she felt any pain.

She yelped like an animal, her howls echoing across the sky, and when she finally looked up, countless uniformed hands gripped shovels, sunken, hollow eyes staring back at her. One pair stood out.

"You will march when called to muster!" shouted the soldier. He held a rifle in the air, his bayonet shining beneath the moonlight. Slowly, the others stabbed their shovels into the dirt, tossing heaps of cold earth one-by-one on top of her.

At dawn, hikers would find a smattering of abandoned supplies next to an empty tent, footprints vanishing into the tree line. This would be the fifth camper to go missing at Cold Harbor Battlefield in as many weeks, but it didn't stop them from coming. Most rationalized the disappearances via a handful of sensible explanations: drugs or accidents, animal attacks or mental health issues, but the locals knew better. If it were opioids or bears, where were the bodies?

Those same locals will warn you that if you see a soldier step from the tree line after dark, you'll know you're late. Don't dare try to desert your place. If you do, the battlefield will claim you, because at Cold Harbor, the dead are always watching, always waiting for the roll to be answered.

# Tour Unit 73Y

## STEPHEN A. RODDEWIG

**Assignment**: *Maintain structural integrity of clients*

**Current Execution Rating**: *Suboptimal*

I would run a few thousand simulations on how that would affect my annual performance review later. Instead, I returned to the task of keeping the mutant coyote's jaws away from the nanomesh material that was my "face."

**Alert**: *Client B vitals spiking*

I turned my head until my "cheek" pressed against the cool stone floor to see her. Ocular sensors, a handicap meant to keep the humans at ease.

Sure enough, Client B—Dr. Lemda—had gotten herself tangled up with a second coyote who decided to move into this place once referred to as Skyline Caverns.

As if you could ever see a skyline *underground*. Man, humans can be stupid.

For example, ignoring my request to hold position.

Not like Client A, who appeared perfectly content to do just that.

I used the Alert to request additional authorizations.

**Enhanced Strength**: *Denied*

**Rationale**: *Clients are unnerved by above-human performance and are unlikely to rehire Unit*

That's me: a perfect weapon forever forced to fight like a human.

I opened the Secondary Menu. Normally useless, but these coyotes were organics. Organics who traced common ancestry to another species quite well studied by humans.

**Enhanced Sonic Range**: *Authorized*

The coyote backing Client B into an alcove froze mid-snarl, ears flattening as it shook its head like it had just inhaled a bad batch of neural static. My own aggressor hesitated, eyes flicking around as sound assaulted it from all directions.

Only a slight reprieve, however. With my human-limited strength, it was possible to beat the mutant coyotes into submission, but I didn't think the clients could spare 4.5 hours.

And the coyotes likely wouldn't go for that, either.

**Arm Cannon**: *Denied*

**Rationale**: *Autocannons fired from palms unnerve—*

Okay, I wasn't authorized for lethals, but Client A had no such parameters.

"Mr. Horne," I called. "Please shoot them."

He mulled it over, then pulled the handgun from its holster.

I wasn't at all surprised when, after expertly firing two laser blasts into Client B's attacker, the barrel drifted toward me.

Two could play at that game. I hooked one arm around the neck of the coyote, just snapping out of its sonic stupor, locked its waist in a vice grip, and heaved it up in front of me as a shield.

The "wild" shots struck it twice. After 1.2 seconds, the man's squishy processor finally caught up.

The belated third shot took off my right arm.

**Arm Cannon**: *Offline*

"Whoops." Client A smirked. "Panicked a bit."

I toggled the pre-recorded response. "It is no problem. I am happy everyone is safe."

Finally, Main System agreed to add a Secondary Threat designation to Client A. Only enough to permit me to anticipate how he might threaten Client B. I couldn't even prepare countermeasures to protect *myself.*

So this is what the humans call "anxiety."

Ahead, the cavern shrunk to a twisting passage sloping downward.

"See the brown line on the wall? This whole passage was filled with mud," Client B said.

Client A snorted. "Archaeologists and mud."

"You wouldn't be so dismissive if you knew anything about anthodites," Client B retorted.

"Just get on with it, Doctor."

"For millions of years, the mud created an airtight seal, preventing oxygen from entering and disrupting the chemical process," Client B said, passing me as she pointed at a white icicle dripping from the ceiling. "These are possibly the most unique crystalline structures on the planet."

"Fascinating." A rustle from behind. "Now retrieve it."

"What—" Client B started to ask. Then her eyes widened.

A glance confirmed he had drawn the handgun.

**Verbal De-escalation**: *Authorized*

"Mr. Horne, take a deep breath—"

"Why don't I just spare you the misery of following your peace-keeping prompts, *tour guide?*"

Crimson light overloaded my ocular sensors, followed by darkness. I felt lighter.

**Head Unit**: *Offline*

Fortunately, that was for show. Putting some of your most vulnerable systems in one exposed mound? Classic humans.

I could still hear them, of course, as I collapsed in a convincing heap.

"Well, now that he— *it* took early retirement, you should get to work, Doctor."

"But... *why?*"

"You think I came all this way for rocks? No. Those crystals are unique, as you said. In fact, it was your open-source scans of them that first alerted my employers to their potential."

"As?"

"Amplifiers. We can use the unique structure to make every energy core on the market today obsolete."

**Alert**: *Core manufacturer directive engaged*

What—

**Prime Directive**: *Protect proprietary company information (power cores)*

**Unit Designation**: *Tour Guide (suspended)*

**Unit Designation**: *Invisible Hand of the Market (engaged)*

**Combat Package**: *Authorized*

This was great and all, but without my ocular sensors—
**Ultra Vision**: *Engaged*

At once, I was inside a 4D rendering of the passage. A tactical combat plan had auto-populated. All I had to do was hand over the controls.

From a prone position, I spun 180 degrees, initiated a somersault bringing me to my feet, seized the gun 0.5 seconds before Primary Threat could begin to pull the trigger, and rotated it so fast it fractured his arm in fifteen different places.

**Primary Threat**: *Neutralized*

But I could still feel the raw power coursing through my system. Surely they'd shut this off as soon as possible.

**Directive**: *Ascertain Client B's intentions*

"Well, that was... equally impressive and terrifying," Client B said behind me.

"Dr. Lemda," I said. "What is your plan for the anthodites?"

"To protect them," she said without hesitation. "We can't have other lunatics coming in here to steal them and lose these precious natural wonders."

**Sincerity Evaluation**: *Genuine*
**New Designation**: *Clueless Egghead*
**Directive**: *Resume normal function*

And just like that, I was seeing out of the backup ocular sensor in my chest. All authorizations revoked.

"Agreed," I said. "Now allow me to escort this particular lunatic out."

It took some doing, considering I only had one arm and Main System only gave me a stingy 30% strength boost. Not to mention, former Client A had passed out from shock—nervous systems have their disadvantages.

Oh well. At least now I had something to look forward to: more would-be crystal thieves and that sweet Combat Package.

# One for the Mountain Folk

## GRACE ATHANASIOU

*Virginia*, Tim thought, watching the state rush past his window, *might be the darkest place in the world*. Mountains rolled past as the car sped down the highway, vague shapes in the night. Every once in a while, the beater's headlights would slam into a highway sign or two. Then they'd be alone again with the road and a sky so thick with stars it looked like spilled salt.

"Look at that." Jerry stifled a yawn. "Rapahammock County."

"Rappahannock, man," Carl admonished. "They don't teach reading at Juilliard?"

Jerry kept his eyes on the road, but punched Carl in the arm. "When you've been driving for four hours straight, you let me know how your vision is. Oh, wait! You can't drive. So how about you just shut up and—"

"Boys, boys, quit fighting," Bill piped up from the backseat, where he was carving his initials into the door with a pocket knife. "Once *The Four Horsemen* get our record deal, we'll get a big old tour bus and hire someone to drive us around. Besides, Jer's the drummer. He doesn't need to know how to read."

Another round of arguments faded into pleasant background noise. Tim was too focused on the sky to think of anything else. Could there really be this many stars? He rolled down the window and leaned out. Cool, misty air ran across his face. He enjoyed it for a moment before a wave of nausea struck and Bill pulled him back in.

"I think Brother Timothy may have overindulged. Stop soon?"

None of them should have been driving at all, if Tim was being honest. They'd played their usual Saturday night gig in Asbury Park until midnight, then piled into Jerry's jalopy. Nashville, land of whiskey and A&R reps. The plan had been to drive straight there until morning, but the adrenaline was wearing off, replaced by the hooks of a nasty hangover.

Tim knew Jerry was tired because he didn't fight. "Alright. But you take the keys, I'm not driving in the morning."

Carl looked out his window. "Okay, boss. Seems to be a nice night for some camping."

So that was how *The Four Horsemen*, Brooklyn's finest new psychedelic rock band, found themselves camping out in the valley of a river that most of them only knew from an old folk song. They stepped over a perfect circle of white mushrooms by the side of the road and shuffled through the wide, flat field until they found a dry patch to lay down.

A combination of exhaustion and the last effects of whatever he took backstage in Jersey washed over Tim. As sleep closed in, a hypnotic clawhammer strum dragged him back to the world of the living.

The rhythmic melody grew louder, closer, until he could hear the accompanying fiddles, spoons, and plaintive voices. Out of the fog at the far side of the field, a throng of people emerged. All wore silver hair that fell to their waists and gossamer robes that shimmered like moonlight on water. They moved in, encircling the Four Horsemen in a wide ring. Their harmonic, lonely song never faltered, even as they completed the circle.

"Some kind of commune?" Bill muttered.

"No," said Jerry. "Older."

A woman stepped forward from the circle. Tim couldn't tell if she was eighteen or eighty, and suspected the question itself was wrong.

*Mountain people,* he thought.

"Mortals, you have entered our territory. We demand a tithe."

As she spoke, the harmonies melted into a screech. Tim jammed his hands over his ears. Next to him, Bill gripped his pocket knife, and Carl fingered the car keys like brass knuckles, the iron keychain dangling by his wrist. Tim's hand found a makeshift weapon in the steel guitar strings in his pocket. None of them would fight unless the strangers jumped them first. Jerry, though, stood and walked toward the woman.

"What the hell are you doing, man?" Tim bellowed.

Jerry didn't blink. "Can't you hear it, Tim? Don't you want to listen?"

As he marched forward, his mouth was slack and his eyes brimmed with tears. The only other time Tim had seen him like that was their eleventh-grade field trip to the Met Opera. Most of the other students were nodding off by the end, but Jerry had been at the edge of his seat, totally enraptured.

In front of Jerry now, the woman lifted her arms, like a ballerina. Like an embrace. Underneath the roar, Tim heard himself and his bandmates screaming. As soon as Jerry touched the woman's hand, the world blinked out, black and silent. Tim's ears rang with the absence of sound.

*** 

Tim's vision blinked back into focus, and he was on his back, staring at a cloudless sky. A figure leaned over him, blocking out the sun. Carl.

"Up and at 'em, Timbo. *Triptych's* future awaits."

Still woozy, Tim hauled himself up to his feet. His utter bewilderment must have been clear on his face, because Carl laughed.

"*Triptych.* You know, the band that started in *your* apartment? Ring a bell?" He knocked on Timothy's head. "You need to lay off the acid, my friend."

Bill slid into the driver's seat. "Nah, Timmy's always been the dreamer in this trio. And the lightest sleeper. You got the whole back to yourself now, man. Get some rest. We'll wake you up when we hit Nashville."

But Jerry had been driving. Jerry, their drummer. Jerry, with the curly black hair and the crooked nose from eighth-grade wrestling, and the *Green Lantern* comic collection. Jerry, his friend.

Tim repeated these things to himself over and over again, for as long as he could, until he could fight sleep no longer. As he drifted off, the enchantment took hold. Memories faded away like mist burning up in the sunrise over the blue ridge of the mountains. In his dreams, the music played on, lonesome and far away, rising from a valley he could never reach.

# Finding Sea Glass

## CAREY ANN MILLER

ON THE DESERTED RIBBON of the Cape Charles beach at low tide, I still managed an awkward collision with a stranger.

Typical of my beach rambles, I had lost track of time and my surroundings, creeping up and down the beach for hours, doubled over, my eyes laser-focused for hidden jewels lodged in the sand.

"Hey there!" A deep voice rumbled into the fog around my brain.

Clutching my bag of treasures to my chest, I lurched wildly into the tall stranger. I had been hunched over in the sun for too long, and my body was as slack as a washed-up jellyfish. Even as he helped steady me, I struggled to focus on him, and my grandmother's gentle voice ping-ponged around in my head.

"Ivy... where are you, my Ivy girl?" Her sweet voice had always coaxed me back when my thoughts wandered, often to imagined places. She had always understood me.

My eyes welled up.

"Hey, are you okay? It's Ivy, right? I didn't mean to scare you. I recognized you from your grandmother's pictures. I'm so sorry about her. I'm Evan Fitzgerald," he added, offering his hand. "Everyone calls me Fitz."

"Oh, Fitzy, her handyman," I nodded, shaking his clean, dry hand before remembering my own hands were caked with beach grit. I studied him. "She mentioned you, but I thought you were older." My grandmother had gone on and on about 'Fitzy,' but I never guessed he was around my age.

He laughed, and the sound breezed through me. I smiled back at him.

"She's the only one who calls me Fitzy, I mean called me Fitzy... jeez. I'm not starting out very good, am I? I've seen your art in her house. The way you incorporate the stuff you find into your pieces is amazing. Find anything good?" His kind, curious eyes stared into mine.

Flattered and flustered, I dug into my bag and held out my prize find, a large piece of amber-colored sea glass, its edges tumbled satin-smooth. From its curve and etchings, I guessed it was the remains of a beautiful old bottle.

"Wow. May I?"

"Of course." I held it out to him.

When he touched the smooth, frosty glass, a current buzzed all the way up my arm. Fitz's eyes widened, as if he felt the jolt too. The sunny sky darkened, and the sand swirled violently around us. Then the air cleared again, heavier now. I stood in a cramped cabin, a wooden plank floor rocking beneath my feet.

I stared into eyes the color of the Chesapeake Bay, familiar to me from a moment ago, but now Fitz's tousled dark hair was longer, and he sported chunky sideburns. His bathing trunks were gone, and he wore a heavy, buttoned-up coat with ruffles at his neck. Our hands were wrapped around a glossy, amber-colored bottle of wine.

"Ivy?" His voice was tentative as he looked me over. My favorite cut-offs and old Richmond Spiders T-shirt had vanished, and I wore a billowy blouse, a heavy long skirt, and sturdy scuffed boots.

"Yes, it's still me," I whispered. "What's happening, Fitz?"

His focus shifted over my shoulder.

"*The Betty?* But how...?" His voice trailed off.

I spun around, my eyes taking in the three portholes and the endless water beyond them. *The Betty* was engraved in scripted gold writing on a plaque above the windows.

"What's *The Betty?*" I asked, afraid of his answer.

"It's the merchant sloop that Blackbeard robbed and sank near Cape Charles in 1717. The crew supposedly dumped crates of Madeira wine into the bay before Blackbeard boarded the ship and stole the rest of the cargo. My great-grandfather nine times back was on that ship; it's legendary in my family. He disappeared after the raid. They told his wife, my ninth great-grandmother, that he joined Blackbeard's crew, but she never believed it and waited out her days in Cape Charles for his return. It's how my family ended up settling here," he explained.

"My grandmother told me an old family story of one of my great-grandfathers escaping pirates by jumping overboard and swimming to shore. She said he came back to Cape Charles years later and built our cottage. I didn't think it was real," I added.

"Ivy, what if your sea glass, which I think is this bottle, was part of that raid, and it brought us here?" He held the bottle of Madeira wine up in the dim light.

It wasn't possible, and yet, here we were.

"If that's true, how do we use it to get back?" I was asking myself as much as Fitz.

"I don't know, but I've studied the old blueprints for this ship. There should be a ladder in the galley up to the main deck. Whatever happens, let's stick together, okay?"

I nodded, terrified but thrilled.

Fitz led the way, bottle in one hand, my hand in his other. We moved as a synchronized team, soundless and stealthy, through the deserted hallways and galley.

Hushed voices drifted towards us when we stepped onto the main deck. We ducked into the shadows to listen.

"I know you're afraid, Thatcher, but we have to jump. You heard Blackbeard. He's not letting us go. It's jump now or join him. You want to see Millie again, don't you?" A smile warmed the man's voice.

"I'm scared," said another voice. "I'm not as brave as you, Fitzgerald. I won't make it in the water."

"You will," the first voice answered. "We'll swim to that lighthouse together."

We stepped out of the shadows. The two men stood poised at the rail, silhouetted in the sun's setting glow. An angry voice barked at them from the other direction.

"You two men, move it this way. Hey, stop there this instant!"

"Thatch, he's got a gun!" Fitzgerald yelled.

He hurled himself at his friend.

A shot exploded.

The bullet struck Fitzgerald; his body jerked hard from the impact, and the momentum carried them both—tangled together—over the rail.

Even as I cried out, Fitz reacted. He scooped me up, crushing me against his body as he vaulted the low railing. I squeezed him back, and we clung together as we plunged into the water after our great-grandfathers.

We were back on the Cape Charles beach an instant later, both soaking wet, staring at each other, the amber piece of sea glass clutched between us.

"What did we just see, Ivy?" Fitz was dazed.

"Fitzy, your great-grandfather didn't join Blackbeard. He saved mine, and I think you just saved me."

I eased the glass gently out of Fitz's clenched fingers, but I didn't let him go. I held his hand tight as we rambled down the beach, our pasts and futures twined together.

# Blue Haze

## JESSICA CARBONI

RUNNING. YOU'RE RUNNING NOW, for what feels like forever. Running till you can't anymore, but you can't stop.

Your breath left you twenty paces back, forgotten as soon as you trekked by that last white blaze. You remember passing it clearly, that simple rectangle of paint on bark, the only thing between you and lost.

Running, but you can't anymore, so you stop, half-stumbling for leverage as your hand latches onto a gnarled nub on the massive oak before you. Its gravity pulls you in and the pounding in your heart begins to ebb, easing second by second. Your grip tightens on that rough bark as if it were the only solid thing still tethering you to sanity.

*Breathe. Remember to breathe.*

Around you, the Blue Ridge folds into itself, hunched shoulders, spine after spine, disappearing into a fogged exhale somewhere behind you, or ahead, or you can't say where exactly, because you've misplaced direction.

When you started your hike, the Priest rose to the north, and though you can't see it anymore, you still sense its heaviness on the horizon, dark and bowed and tired of shouldering the sky.

You read all the lore before setting out. You did your research. The area featured a cluster of peaks some called the Religious Range: the Priest, the Friar, the Cardinal, and so on.

Oh, how you laughed at the names when you read the trail guide.

That was a day ago.

That was a different you.

The you who came out here to prove something, or rather, to prove that something didn't exist. *@wanderingskeptic*, out here hiking the trails for content. Phone in hand, coupled with ever-ready smiles of ironic commentary, you came here ready to debunk these supposedly haunted, ancient trails: "So apparently you're not supposed to whistle out here, let's see what happens."

You picked the area specifically for its mysterious true-crime material. The unsolved homicide from 2011 with its hiker found in a shallow grave, death by asphyxiation, no suspects, case still open. Or that other hiker who vanished in 2019. His wallet turning up months later near... well, near here, maybe right here, where you're standing.

Eventually, his body was found...

You find yourself wishing you hadn't thought about those facts at all.

At the time, they were grim, sure, but great content. But now, you're alone, clinging to a tree trunk, and as those same facts pop into your mind, you pair each flash of paranoia with the cycling mantra of: "don't think, don't think, don't think."

You're a skeptic. You doubt this chant will save you. Do you need saving? *Have we come to that?! No, no! Think of happier thoughts...*

The trail was stunning.

You remember that too, and the remembering aches. Cole Mountain's bald summit finally cracked open after more than two hours in the forest's dense tree-tunnel. The shock of witnessing that late-afternoon sky, the golden burnt grass rippling in the wind, made the world feel enormous. The patchwork of fields stitched up between ridges, and the ruddy-colored valleys bleeding away into the blue haze, you stopped to film it all, saying for the camera: "See? Just more trees. Just mountains. The only horror is my stunned face at how beautiful it is out here."

Then, there was the descent, and the world closed in.

Your footsteps stopped echoing; sound doesn't carry the same way down in the hollows. It gets swallowed.

The ground softened beneath your boots like you wandered into the memory of centuries, called back in the ghostly scent of wet earth, slow rot, duff and decay.

That scent followed you off the trail, and even here, it lingers as you cling to this one of many majestic oaks as if it were a ward-marker keeping you safe. You are the interloper here, like it was *you* who agitated something where nothing has been disturbed in a long, long time...

The rules! All at once, you remember. *Don't whistle at night. Don't answer if you hear your name. Don't look too hard into the trees.* You broke them one by one for the amusement of your audience and the entertainer in yourself, the fool-version that believed knowing the trick meant the trick was harmless.

However, with each new tick in the box of transgressions, you couldn't *not* notice the air change. You could have convinced yourself that it was just the arriving evening, but even that couldn't explain the *texture* of it, like the woods changed their breathing, turning their attention toward you, slowly, stirring before waking.

You kept walking, though, despite that feeling. Kept walking, kept filming until you followed a curious maybe-noise and stepped off the marked path. Just a few steps really, until the oppressive quiet was too much to bear, and you turned back, only to find that the last white blaze wasn't where you left it. Two trees you'd just passed stood in different positions, you swear they were or... you imagined their positions wrong or... the forest was, is, rearranging itself while you aren't looking.

You inhale in a deep, shuddering breath. In any case, your phone is dead and you're here, gripping this oak, and can finally hear past the pounding blood in your ears. The shelter is maybe half a mile away—

Behind you, a branch snaps.

Breathing. Someone breathing, getting closer. You should move. You should run. The breathing becomes louder, gasping and ragged. Here's the prickling at the back of your neck, here's the creeping up your spine. You should run. You're going to run now. You can't stand it, not for another second, the dread, the almost-here.

*You should run, run, run, just go, go now, go, now—*
*RUN!*

Running. You're running now, for what feels like forever. Running till you can't anymore, but you can't stop.

# The Sirens of Chesapeake

## DAVID HORN

THE SKIFF ROCKED SOFTLY on the gray-green water, crab pots piled high like stacks of iron cages against the gunwale. Jonah, the youngest deckhand, squatted beside them, inspecting a frayed line with his mittened fingers reddened by cold. A gull circled above him, screaming like a spear piercing the dawn silence. Purple and slate, storm clouds bruised the horizon. Copper and salt lay heavy on the morning air.

Eli squinted at the sky. "Nor'easter's coming early," he muttered, twisting the throttle. The engine coughed once, then settled into a low growl. "We'll haul quick and head in."

Beside him, Mason leaned over the side, fingers trailing in the brackish water. The Bay was warmer than it should have been, almost oily.

"Did you hear that?" he said through clenched teeth.

Eli frowned. "Hear what?"

Something called them through the wind. It was thin and musical, almost human. It swooped and dipped like inhalation and exhalation—too rhythmic to be the ocean. Eli thought it was wind whistling through the sails, but the notes were intentional, curling around smoke.It swelled into a chorus; voices weaving together like reeds in water. Eli heard fragments float toward him—syllables plaited with haunting pitches, ancient and unfamiliar.

Mason tensed and stared at the water ahead. "That's Algonquian," he breathed. "My grandma used to tell me stories. They said Powhatan spirits drowned when colonists arrived. Watched over the Bay—the ones who couldn't make it across. The ones who were stolen."

Eli snorted, but it came out dry. "Ghost stories to keep kids from drowning." He'd heard them all his life: tales of the "water-women" who could suck a man's breath from ten feet away, of lights on the water that lured boats to their doom, of the unending hunger of the Bay itself. But this was different. This sound had teeth.

The water shimmered, but not with reflected light. From within it came a glow, phosphorescent but not artificial. Underwater, shapes drifted in the mottled surface. Hair streamed like eelgrass; eyes glowed faintly with the foxfire of decaying flesh. They weren't mermaids from fairy tales, all curves and smiling faces. These were children of the deep, skin the pale mottled green of a river stone, fingers long and webbed. One rose until her face broke the skin of the sea, lips moving in time with the song. Her voice lapped like tide over stones, soft and insistent.

"Tribute," she said, the word a bubble of air and sound. "Before the storm."

Eli's knuckles whitened on the wheel. The compass needle swung lazily, pointing to nothing. "What the hell...!"

The siren lifted an arm, pointing east. Black clouds devoured the sun, and the wind sharpened to an edge. The smell of ozone burned Eli's nose, thick as the cloying scent of marsh decay.

"What do they want?" Mason hissed. "Money? Fish?"

The boat lurched as waves, born from nowhere in the flat sea, slapped the hull. Rain stung like needles. The sirens circled, weaving a net of sound through the water that vibrated in the wood, in Eli's teeth. His breath came fast.

"We give them the catch," he said, hauling a bushel of crabs and tossing it overboard. The shells clattered like bones on the deck before they hit the water.

The sirens' laugh sounded like breaking glass, like ice cracking on a frozen pond.

"Not enough," they chorused, voices a dissonant chord of hunger and ancient grief. "Your metal is cold. Your catch is soulless. The Bay wants warmth. It wants memory."

Lightning forked across the sky, silent and blinding. The engine sputtered and died, leaving only the song and the rising wind. Mason gripped Eli's arm, face ashen.

"They'll sink us. They'll drag us down to the lost towns, the ones the water claimed."

Eli swallowed hard, throat thick with salt and fear. "What else can we give?"

The youngest deckhand, Jonah, stared at the storm, lips trembling. He was only nineteen, but his grandmother's eyes, dark and deep.

"My grandma said they want remembrance," he murmured, his voice nearly lost in the gale. "A life for a life. A name to be spoken on the water. They're the ones who were forgotten. They don't want to kill us. They just don't want to be alone anymore."

Before Eli could stop him, Jonah whispered a prayer in the same strange, liquid syllables the sirens used. He vaulted the rail. The sea swallowed him whole, not with a crash, but with a sigh, as if it had been waiting.

The sirens surged, eddying around him in a halo of foam. Their song swelled, sweet and terrible, as the storm began to ease. Jonah's silhouette faded into the depths, arms outstretched not like a crucifix, but like an embrace. For a moment, the water glowed with a soft, internal light, and the song was no longer a command but a lullaby of welcome.

The Bay smoothed to glass. Rain softened to mist. The sirens sank without a ripple, their voices receding to a hum that tasted of grief and salt.

Eli stared at the empty deck, heart hammering against his ribs like a trapped bird. Mason wiped his face with a shaking hand, smearing salt and tears across his cheeks.

"We'll tell no one," he said, voice raw. "They'll say we were drunk. That Jonah fell."

A single crab pot floated by, severed from its rope with a single, sharp bite. From the deep came a whisper, almost tender, that only Eli seemed to hear: We'll return when the Bay forgets again.

Eli turned the skiff toward shore, the words echoing through his skull. The old saying rang true at last. No debt to the Bay was settled in coin or catch—only in stories, in names, and in warmth given to the cold, forgotten deep. And he knew, with a certainty that chilled him more than the storm, that the Bay had a long memory and a bottomless hunger—and that the Chesapeake keeps its debts.

# Leave No Trace

## ALEX TUCKER

BELIEVE IT OR NOT, the Appalachians are among the oldest mountains in the world. When compared to the Rockies, the eastern range might seem little more than rolling hills, but the latter has nearly a half-billion more years under its belt. In Virginia, the Blue Ridge Mountains once dominated the ancient skies. Although eons of erosion have dwindled them to what we know today, the evidence is still there—if you know where to look.

Behind the house where my Mamaw and Papaw still live, there's a point known around Lee County as Buzzard's Roost. While it might not be as tall as the peaks of Cumberland Gap or the High Knob, the hike is quite demanding. Every time my sister and I made the trek as kids, we each packed a light lunch. Otherwise, it meant several hours with nothing more than some wild crab apples.

The best part was the fossils. Every rock we flipped over was a thumbprint left behind, detailing the geological age of those hills. We'd find seashells in them, despite standing hundreds of miles from the Atlantic Ocean. Other aquatic critters were also embedded in these stones, frozen for our curious minds to inspect. Some were rather unusual, including one that appeared to be a mix of a starfish and squid. We had to assume it had become extinct at some point. On every trip up there, I'd bring back at least one specimen for my growing collection.

These relics of the earth were precious to me, and I treated them like delicate newborn kittens. I've never so much as cracked or chipped these preserved remains of ancient life, and when I learned what happened in all those cities around the country, I was beyond grateful for that fact.

After Mamaw and Papaw finally retired from farming, some middleman from New York struck a deal with them to extract and haul away the large boulders embedded in the mountainside. Apparently, the company behind it was turning around and selling them to hotels and other businesses who wanted to decorate their lobbies with natural stones. We all found it sort of funny, having grown up seeing these things everywhere we turned. But we weren't about to question free money.

From late spring to early fall that year, the operation went off without a hitch. The contractors shut it down before the cold weather set in, with plans to restart the following year. My grandparents enjoyed the break from all the commotion. No one could've known it would become a permanent one.

The first report came out of Nashville, where one of our boulders had been installed in the lobby of a ritzy hotel known as The Winstead. The interior designers had set it up with a steady stream flowing over the rock face, down into a small pool where the water was recirculated. The fountain was lovely and peaceful until the water started turning blue.

Obviously, water is often known to contain some shade of blue—whether natural or unnatural—so the change was initially disregarded. Perhaps some cleaning chemical had been added, or someone had dyed it for effect. When the phenomenon was finally investigated, potential causes like these were quickly eliminated—and yet the water remained tainted. Several days passed before someone from the city health department put a sample under a microscope. By then, it was too late.

The same occurrence was reported in Cincinnati, then Richmond, then Philadelphia, which was when the CDC became involved. In a matter of weeks, blue water was flowing in hotels and conference centers across the country.

Next came the illnesses.

Whatever was in the fountains had leapt, swam, and flowed until it found its way into the local water systems, allowing microscopic colonies to form and spread across the cities. The water became diluted, masking the blue coloring by the time it poured from every kitchen sink. It must've tasted fine, too. Then again, just one gulp was a death sentence. Even a shower wasn't safe.

The contaminant no longer had a single source, having migrated to the wells, springs, reservoirs, and sewers. The microorganisms were thriving and reproducing as if they'd always been there. The rare, lucky survivors lived off bottled water for a while, but eventually they had to be evacuated. The unseen organisms own those cities now.

As a geologist—thanks to those early days on Buzzard's Roost—I find it takes all my willpower to resist conducting an investigation of my own. Others have, and I've benefited from their published findings. However, more than half of those scientists are now dead. What I've learned from their brief successes couldn't hold a candle to their permanent mistakes.

In truth, we might not ever understand the nature of that blue microscopic life. It hails from a time long before humans existed, a time we can only speculate in our textbooks and scientific papers. We've only recently—in relative terms—unlocked the secrets to protecting ourselves against *modern* pathogens and viruses. Our new foe is deadlier and more mysterious than anything ever encountered, resetting our immunological clock back to zero.

We have only ourselves to blame. Had we followed the old adage "Leave No Trace", we would've left those mountains alone. We wouldn't have tampered with their skeletons like twisted surgeons, releasing a rot that festers in our own bones.

Perhaps we can still learn from this failure. We must leave the mountains as they are, protect them as I protected those fossils in my collection. The Appalachians are more than just a home to gorgeous wildlife, because they're also a prison, holding back a lethal threat against *all* life. If we keep the remaining stones sealed, nothing more can escape.

Of course, this ignores the very nature of water.

How long do we really think we have?

# Rubilacxe

GRIFF THOMAS

"WHERE'D YOU GET THAT, Chef?"

"That, Chef?"

"The knife?"

"Oh, that. Ordered it on QVC."

"QVC, you say?"

"Yep. You need a good tomato knife when you're fixin' a meal."

"Now, hold on, I ain't talkin' about that one."

"Well, now, no need to get testy, fella."

"I ain't gettin' testy. I'm tryin' to figure out your particular brand of bewilderment."

"Whoa there, slow down. Give a man a chance to think. What did you say?"

"Where'd I lose ya?"

"Right after, 'where'd you get that?'"

"I see you with that same set of knives you always carry."

"Like you've seen me with many, many times."

"Yep."

"The tomato knife's one of 'em, ain't it?"

"Sure as Adam."

"And I've seen it."

"You bet."

"But now, you got yourself another one—somethin' I ain't seen before."

"Oh, you mean the long-handled one."

"Yep. The very same."

"It's new."

"Now we're gettin' somewhere."

"Well... new to me, anyway."

"How do you mean?"

"Well, it's actually ancient, I reckon. It's got funny writin' all over it. Can't read a lick of it, but I was thinkin' maybe it's written in Canadian."

"Ain't nobody speaks Canadian."

"Since when?"

"Since always, friend. What I mean to say is, there never was a language called Canadian."

"I'm as mortified as a hound guardin' the privy."

"Truly, you have a colorful way of talkin'. What's written on that long knife?"

"Like I said, I can't read that Canadian—or whatever it is."

"Can you make out what the letters or symbols are?"

"R-U-B-I-L-A-C-X-E."

"What kind of word is that?"

"Engraved."

"I'm much obliged for you reinforcin' the obvious. Can you read it the other way?"

"It still don't make no sense."

"Spell 'em out anyway, son."

"E-X-C-A-L-I-B-U-R."

"Excalibur. Where on Earth did you find this knife?"

"Up on Mount Rogers, on the Rhododendron Trail."

"The Appy Trail? What in tarnation were you doin' way up there?"

"Breathing the fresh air. Watchin' the wild ponies. They're right pretty."

"And you found this knife there?"

"Mm-hmm. As far as I can figure, they was havin' one of those whatchamacallit fairs, you know—"

"A Renaissance Fair?"

"Exactly! I reckon some poor soul was tryin' to sharpen the long-handled knife and somehow got it stuck smack-dab in the middle of a great big granite boulder they got up there. Folks was lined up all day, payin' five dollars a chance to pull it out. I thought they were loco."

"Are you sure this wasn't a dream you was havin'?"

"This was as real as it gets. I thought it strange myself, but who can account for what folks do these days? A lot of them looked like they were a little off their rocker."

"Not me."

"Anyway, when it got dark, folks scattered, leaving me and a few others up there. I was gettin' hungry, so I got myself a fire goin', heated my cast-iron skillet, and got out my ingredients. I had everything simmerin', and it smelled amazin'. All I needed was to cut my vegetables, but I'd left my knives at home. Then, I remembered the knife in the rock and gave the thing a good yank, and it came right out—sent me flying on my backside. That knife sliced those vegetables like hot butter, and I ain't made a meal without it since. It sure is a pretty thing."

"You know what you've got there, don't you?"

"Why, of course, I do. I just told you, it's like a Ginsu steak knife with a long handle."

"It's a little more than that—"

"It's got a pretty gold handle with little flying dragons engraved on it. Both sides sharp as can be, and the handle's made of bone. The weird thing is, it looks like it oughta be heavy, but it's light as a feather."

"Well, I'll be. Now, I ain't positive, but I'd say you're usin' Excalibur, the most famous sword in history, to prep your vegetables."

"Well, what's wrong with that? It works great."

"You could be the king!"

"Of where?"

"England!"

"No way!"

"Yes way!"

"I ain't really lookin' to be King of England. Not much of a tea man. I like coffee."

"Think of the history of the thing!"

"It's just a big knife."

"Too big to keep in your knife roll."

"Honestly, the blade is a tad long for juliennin' vegetables. What am I supposed to do, become a butcher? I'm a chef! Besides, I already got a Slap Chop."

"A fella can't discard a once-in-a-lifetime kitchen item like that."

***

*Forty years later.*

"That's quite a story, Chef."

"I had to make a tough choice, Chef, and frankly, the Slap Chop won out. It chops anything from onions to nuts. And the handle on the Excalibur is a beast. The blade is a beast. This thing has a beastly feel, and I don't feel like cookin' with a beast anymore."

"When is your yard sale?"

"This weekend. Gotta get rid of some junk before the move. Stop by, this thing's going for cheap. Maybe some young'un could use it for a Halloween costume."

The following Saturday, there it was, a hand-painted sign on a post reading:

**Yard Sale! Everything 50% Off! Antiques, Tools, Collectibles & Misc.**

And right in the middle of the driveway, propped against a cardboard box overflowing with old Tupperware and broken kitchen gadgets, was a magnificent golden-handled sword. A little handwritten sticky note was affixed to the blade:

**Old Sword. Works great. No returns. $5.**

# Rebirth

## ARRE SHANE

I turn sideways, slipping through the chevron-shaped crack, banging my helmet against the rock in the process. I hear myself say ouch even though it doesn't hurt. I wonder how Spence squeezed through at twice my size.

I scuttle through another narrow opening, the passage expanding into a small chamber. Lana is shining her headlamp toward some bats clustered on the far wall, saying something to Spence, who seems recovered from the motion sickness he experienced through the Highland County switchbacks. I resolve not to sit next to him in the van on the trip back.

Lana turns her headlamp to a crawlway near the cavern floor. "This part isn't bad". She descends gracefully into the opening. Spence follows. Josh just stands there, hiding behind his beard and tinted glasses. I can't see his eyes, but imagine them crawling all over me.

I shudder and gesture toward the opening. "After you". He shrugs and drops into the hole. I'm next, leaving only Sophia behind me. She is the TA for my intro geology course, and the one who invited me here after a class trip to Grand Caverns. I wonder if we'll be friends.

The tunnel roof scrapes my back, so I sink to my elbows and splay my knees outward and behind, thankful that Josh isn't behind me. Stones dig into my forearms, but then the roof pulls away and I'm able to lift myself into something resembling a bear crawl.

The second pinch is tighter, but the mud along the bottom is forgiving. I'm getting the hang of it and reflexively fight back a smile as I pull myself into a limestone cathedral.

"The mirror room", Lana says, as I move toward the reflective pool near the center.

I stand near the edge and take in my reflection. I've acquired a new mole on my cheek, and I wipe it with the back of a gloved hand, but it is persistent. The glove smells faintly of Lysol.

Lana, who started caving as a little girl in Slovenia and is the president of JMU's caving club, glances over. "My Nona thought these pools were places where the boundary between the living and the dead is thin."

A drop of water plops into the pool, ripples radiating outward, distorting the surface. My reflection morphs into something malevolent, and I back away more quickly than I intend. The name "Casey" rises in my mind, unbidden.

Lana smiles gently. "When my Nona was a girl, they explored by candlelight. Much creepier, I would think." She turns to illuminate an opening that contracts quickly into not much. "So who's ready to enter the birth canal?"

I begin on hands and knees but soon can only frog crawl. No space to bring my arms back to my sides, and I begin to feel things closing in, the smell of damp earth becoming vaguely threatening. I find myself practicing a breathing technique I learned in therapy years ago—five in, hold for five, five out—and the panic spiral slowly subsides. I'm moving again.

After some minutes, the tunnel turns sharply straight down. My headlamp reveals the floor of what appears to be a larger chamber a few feet away. If I bend at the waist, I might reach the bottom with my hands to lower myself. I shimmy forward into a sort of headfirst plunge and immediately start to slip. My helmet is ripped away and drags behind me, straps tightening around my neck. I try in vain to reach the floor with my hands. My vision narrows, and I recognize that I am about to pass out. Fortunately, I start sliding again and am expelled from the opening, landing on my side with a thud.

As I catch my breath and start to rise, Spence's light falls on me. "Welcome to the delivery room, Sami."

Once Sophia arrives, Lana gathers us. Her nose scrunches. "We usually spend an hour or so in total darkness here—the mind doesn't like empty spaces and will try to fill them—some people experience pretty intense visuals, others deep contemplation. Do whatever works for you."

We find comfortable places to recline, and the headlamps go out. Conversation fades more slowly than light, but soon we find both darkness and silence. Time passes strangely. Purple and green blotches appear in my field of vision, pulsing and shifting. Two long, uneven purple cables manifest and intertwine into a tight double helix. Black patches bloom on one and it begins to shrivel. I find myself thinking about a story one of my cousins told me when we were ten. Seems that my aunt knew someone who was carrying twins, but the umbilical cords became entangled, and only one of the twins was born alive.

Another time when I was six or seven, I discovered a circular tin in my mother's closet. A baby's footprint in ink. A tooth. A tiny pink hospital bracelet, cut. An ultrasound photograph that I didn't understand. Two names scrawled on an index card. Samantha Marie, and one I don't remember. I asked my mother about it once—she said they had two names picked out for me and didn't decide which to use until I was born. A few years later, I spent half a day looking for that tin, but couldn't find it again.

A phone alarm goes off, and headlamps cut the darkness. We walk through a passageway leading to the exit, quietly, seemingly content to remain in our pockets of isolation for a bit longer. The sunlight is cruelly bright as we leave the cave and stagger toward the van.

I crawl toward the back and curl up in a corner seat. The other name comes to me—it was Katherine Corrine. K.C., I realize suddenly. Gravel crunches as the van pulls onto Burnsville Road. My mind starts filling in the empty spaces.

# The Bakery by Campus

ALEXIS COLLINS

Elizabeth's window in Webb Hall frosted over with the scent of hot, freshly baked bread. This happened every morning at six o'clock, the cracks of the old dorm letting in curls of steam. Normally, Elizabeth resisted the temptation, but this December day, she dressed in the dark so as not to disturb her roommate, throwing on layer after layer, and slipped out the door.

Most first years, like herself, assumed the smell of bread was a hallucination or just the dining hall preparing breakfast. The older students never mentioned it.

"It's bad luck to talk about it," a junior hissed at Elizabeth when she dared to bring it up. The older students believed an awful number of things were bad luck, including walking through Mary's Garden before you graduated and entering the engagement tower before you were engaged. But Elizabeth liked hearing about history—superstitions, ghost stories, traditions and all.

As she crossed campus, it was like wading through fog. Despite the dark, only pierced by the eerie blue light of the emergency towers, her feet knew the sloping brick pathways well.

Margaret's Gate punctured the red brick wall before her. The wall encircled Randolph College in a half-hearted hug, dividing the road from the limits of campus. As soon as Elizabeth murmured to Margaret and stepped through the gate, she felt herself being peeled away from the bubble of campus.

She groggily wrapped her scarf tighter around her neck. As she followed the scent of baked bread, her breath misted the air like kettle steam. She took the crosswalk—because even half asleep, she wasn't uncivilized—and passed the boutique shops dotting each side of Rivermont Avenue.

The bakery by campus was only blocks away. In the frosted air, Elizabeth's head cleared, and she realized that the bakery was probably haunted—but no more haunted than the rest of campus.

Ghost stories crawled over the grounds like the ivy snaking over the red brick wall. The abandoned fourth floor of Main Hall carried oppressively heavy air, and deep into the night, the piano in Presser played by itself. There was the murdered Clog Girl, who was the heir to the Hellmann's Mayonnaise Company; the woman who haunted the mirror in the West Dating Parlor; the student who either fell or was pushed down one of the spiraling staircases called the curlies; and an actor who died in a car crash that haunted the theater in Smith Hall.

Elizabeth followed the glowing rings of the street lamps, her boots the only sound other than the rogue car puttering along the pavement. The scent grew stronger, permeating her brain, and she took a sharp right as the bakery emerged, its sign stamped with *Lynchburg Bakery* swinging silently.

She pushed open the door. Stepped into warm, fluorescent light. A bell above her rattled, startling her.

"Welcome," said a smooth voice.

Elizabeth blinked the darkness from her eyes and saw a woman behind the checkout counter, rolling dough with her gloved hands, the back-and-forth motion hypnotizing.

In her mittens, Elizabeth's hands began to sweat.

Behind the counter, a flurry of shapes moved back and forth in time with the rolling, and Elizabeth squinted.

"You can see them, then?" The baker paused in her rolling. "I suppose you wouldn't be here if you couldn't."

Elizabeth rubbed her eyes. "I—I can't quite—"

The baker plucked a pastry from the case. She held it out in her palm.

Elizabeth took off one of her mittens, padded forward, and accepted an apple turnover. Then she crunched into it, steam curling against the roof of her mouth.

The baker lifted her eyebrows. "Better?"

"It's very good." Elizabeth looked up to see the fuzzed shapes solidify into something half-corporeal.

The baker smiled and slid back behind the counter, where she continued to roll the dough.

Behind the baker, the ghosts stood in a circle. Their mouths moved, yet the bakery was silent but for the rolling and the buzzing of the light overhead, and in their wavering hands, they each held a pastry, the steam filtering through their hazy bodies.

Elizabeth still held the turnover in her bare hand. "What are they doing?"

The baker didn't look up from her task. "Eating, of course."

Slowly, Elizabeth took another bite, and the ghosts sharpened. One of them wore clogs, and when she swiveled her head, she revealed a face that looked like a melting ice sculpture. Another ghost's neck crooked sideways, yet she smiled and laughed as she ate the pastry and talked to an older woman in a long dress. The last was a young man dressed in a Shakespearean costume, hat bobbing as he ate.

"You need to escort them back," said the baker. "They prefer to be *escorted.*"

Elizabeth blinked. "Back?"

"To campus, of course." The baker began slicing the dough into triangles. "When they're done eating, Randolph will call them back."

She was right; as soon as the pastries disappeared, the ghosts glided through the checkout counter to cluster around Elizabeth. The back of her neck prickled. The older woman only reached for her hand, and the ghostly touch burned freezing cold across Elizabeth's skin.

As the ghosts ushered her out the door, Elizabeth waved to the baker. "I'll be back, won't I?"

The baker's smile flickered. "Some come back. Some don't. It all depends on if you remember."

Outside, the ghosts shone a pearly blue under the ebbing light of the moon. When Elizabeth stepped through Margaret's Gate, a string of whispers stuffed her ears, and the ghosts slipped after her as a flurry of snowflakes swept the air.

# Trail Magic

## MaryJune Haines

THE RV APPEARED ON the grass beside the road on a Monday, my day off, the day and night I spent at home with the little one. So it wasn't until Tuesday that I started driving past it, coming through Dooms. Five times I went past it, glancing a little longer at each pass, thinking of what we could do with it if we had it.

No price listed. Only a laminated sign jammed into the grass: *For Sale by Owner.*

*Sandpiper* swirled in script on its side.

The sixth time, coming home, I pulled off where the gravel met the grass and got out to take a look. My eyes itched when I swiped pollen from a window to peer inside. Clean inside, but old. Older than me—ancient to the little one—though beggars couldn't be choosers. Our lease was ending, and I was about to be out of a job. The café would close soon, no matter the owners' optimism. Walk-up business languished despite its prime spot downtown. Haunted by its own potential, or maybe, the rent was just too high. Nothing to do with ghosts at all.

And the summer was almost over.

With this new ride, our time here could be over, too.

I remembered Dad's old camper, sitting high in the bucket seat while he handled the wide steering wheel. The little one wasn't around then. She came later, before Dad's heart attack, picked up in Pennsylvania as a curious piece of cargo. *Where's her mama?* I asked Dad, and he shrugged and said, *She's half an orphan but we'll love her, won't we?* I was no good then at telling a kid's age;

all I knew was that she was small, and silent, and dreamed very deep at night.

I could take her out of this nowhere town. Rescind my application to the Waffle House. I couldn't afford another place just the two of us, anyway. There would never be anything cheaper than the shoebox I'd found two Septembers ago. Even there, the hole in the hallway floor got wider and deeper with every step we took around it, and there was always a line of ants trailing in from the kitchen windowsill.

I imagined autumn in New England: crisp and cool, orange-and-red leaves scattered out to sea. I'd had friends there once, years ago. School began later in New England. The little one wouldn't miss any. If she did, she could read on the road. A six-year-old could play anywhere, and she could read anything anywhere. She was smarter than I'd ever been.

"Are you interested?"

I startled.

An old woman, come from the house behind the RV, where I couldn't see her, put up her hands and smiled. "Did I frighten you? I'm sorry."

"I might be," I answered her first question. "Interested. How much?"

"Make me an offer." The woman's hair was silver-blond, frizzled in the sun, her skin glistening.

I didn't know about that. "Is there anything wrong with it?"

"Not a thing."

"Why're you selling it?"

"It was my husband's. He was a big hiker, camper. After he retired, he would drive this thing up to where the Appalachian Trail crossed with Skyline Drive and hand out trail magic. Do you know—?"

"I know trail magic."

"Well, he died a year ago. Up in Shenandoah, actually, in… well, if you can believe it." The woman smiled and shrugged. "I have no use for it now. It was his hobby, not mine."

I nodded. "Can I see the inside?"

"Of course." The old woman unlocked the door and held it open for me, but did not come in herself. "I'll go check my mailbox while you have a look," she said. "Take your time."

The interior was very clean, the surfaces dustless, polished, the bed turned down invitingly. There was a slight odor that I couldn't place—an earthiness, muskiness, almost like decaying leaves but less pleasant. After a few minutes of looking, I was already sorting our life into piles in my head: Keep; Donate; Throw Away. Our shoebox was small; this RV was even smaller.

I couldn't make an offer, not without the little one's approval, but I asked if I could come back tomorrow.

"Of course," she said. I wanted her to get inside, too, because the sweat stains under her arms were enormous and her forehead dripped. She'd been twisting her mail between her hands.

***

The next day, I didn't tell the little one where we were going. She knew Dooms only as a corridor between places. So when I pulled the truck over, she looked at me curiously.

The old woman met us, waving.

"Come look inside," I said to the little one. She held my hand tight. She didn't acknowledge the old woman. I let her climb inside ahead of me.

Again, the old widow stayed outside.

I let the little one explore the RV for herself. In the small bedroom, she stopped and then shuddered.

Like one yawn following another, I shivered, too. That faint odor rose again in my nostrils, sweet but not pleasant.

"Wouldn't it be perfect, baby?" I said.

"No."

I frowned. "No?"

"Can we go?" Her little voice was a whisper. I turned her to face me and saw that her big doe eyes were glassy with unshed tears. "*Please*," she whispered. Her pulse ticked in her throat.

I wanted to say, *No. This is our way out.* I'd already emptied my savings account, everything Dad had left for us, to whisk her away in this home on wheels. The wad of cash burned a hole in my pocket.

I swallowed. "Okay. We'll say no."

On the drive home, I looked at her from the corner of my eye. Her lips quivered. Her chin wobbled. She sniffed but was otherwise silent.

Finally, I asked, "Baby, what is it?"

The tears came then, rolling fat down her cheeks. "Didn't you *see* him?"

# Move to the Country, They Said, It'll be Relaxing, They Said...

## JEN POTEET

**(Based on a True Piedmont Haunting)**

SUMMER HEAT LINGERS INTO fall, the Piedmont Virginia temperatures not ranging too far off from where we moved. I fell in love with the two-story white farmhouse with the red door as soon as I laid eyes on it-despite the mulberry tree growing in the front yard, its discarded fruit rotting underfoot. I pay no mind to the stench nor the incessant hum of insect wings. I've dreamed of this lifestyle change and slower living. It will do us good.

The house was built in the late 1800s, right after our country sent boys to war to fight each other. Matter of fact, an actual battlefield sits across the road. The land is protected from development by the state to honor the blood that was spilt there. Concrete markers commemorating noteworthy deaths jut from the overgrown wooded trails like broken bones. Both sides claimed at least two hundred losses between them—at least there's a plaque proclaiming so. Soldiers must have walked our rental property too, maybe they even died on it.

Unpacking didn't take long, we downsized too. Less space, less stuff, less stress. The Blue Ridge Mountains lay across the sky, watching me tend the small garden I planted next to a henhouse. Around the time my damp hair sticks to my neck, I head inside to escape the heat. The air inside is almost as heavy. I can't explain it, but it feels like someone laid their coat on my shoulders, and an unseen weight hovers there.

Bored, I sweep. The broom's fibers stick in the uneven floorboards. I don't fuss, these floors have character. "What was that?" I say to no one but myself, I thought I heard a shuffle in the front room.

The lights flicker. On. Off. On. Off. In a structure this old, there has got to be a faulty wire or two. The house has stood so long, faulty or not, it must not be a fire hazard. Another thing I hadn't considered when moving into a historic home.

Every morning when I enter the kitchen, the cabinets are open wide. The foundation must have settled, and the house sits on a lean. I contemplate getting something to latch them but don't want to risk my security deposit. I close the doors again and again. My son won't go in there. He asks me to get him snacks.

When I ask him why, he says, "I don't like the floating lights." It's daytime and I don't see a thing.

***

"Do you ever feel weird here?" I ask my husband as we sit on the porch drinking tea one evening. We rock in chairs like old folks, soaking in the sounds of the night. The noises coming from the battlefield aren't what I'd call soothing though.

"Not really, but what do think is making that?" he replies. "A fox?"

I'm not sure why, but I don't think it's a fox, and I don't think I want to find out either way.

***

I wonder if my imagination is in overdrive. In addition to the lights and cabinets, footsteps stomp daily up and down the staircase. My ears perk up at a shuffle in the hall. If I look, I may find answers to the questions that I don't want to acknowledge. Foolishness wins, I can't resist. When I peek around the corner toward the noise, I see it, only a shadow. Details are blurry, but one thing is for certain, like I had feared, we didn't move into an empty house.

***

As I step from my shower, I get the feeling I am being watched. My head swivels left and right in the cramped space. I wipe away condensation from the medicine cabinet mirror. Terror fills my body as another face is reflected in the glass. Slowly I turn to look, but there is nothing between me and the door.

***

No one else sees him.

I wonder if rural life has driven me to madness instead of the solace I'd come here to seek. The lights still flick on and off, the cabinets gape wide open, footsteps continue to sound, and in my peripheral vision there is a man dressed in a uniform from days past. There are months left on our lease, so I console myself. At least that thing keeps some distance. At least it just opens cabinets and flicks on lights. At least, at least... it hasn't touched me. Yet.

I gaze out the window above the deep sink as I hand wash dishes. Between our yard and the mountains stretches a feed field, the tall stalks of hay wave in a breeze. There is a touch of cool air on the back of my neck, the hair there stands on end. Unrecognizable words are whispered into the shell of my ear. My flesh pebbles. A soft pressure at my hip. A phantom squeeze. "Oh, hell no." My stomach plummets. I spew vomit onto the clean plates, cups and utensils. Lease or not, I can't stay in this house any longer.

***

I collect mail from the box at our new address. The air is not heavy with what I now recognize as a ghost in the room. The air is just air. The rental company has sent us a letter.

"What now?" I mumble as I tear open the envelope, they already kept our deposit for breaking the lease. Apparently "haunted" isn't a good enough reason to do so. They're billing us for trashing the house when we moved out. The bathroom mirror is smashed, and scratches are gouged in the red door on the inside from our dog. Pictures are enclosed. I feel the unnaturalness from here. I'll pay the fine.

They wouldn't believe me even if I told them... we never had a dog.

# The Grit in the Baseboards

## SHANNON WAGONER

RAINDROPS FELL THROUGH THE hole that erased the line between inside and outside. Sun shone through it on rainless days, and dry wind crept through each crack in the house. Day after day my green flecks thickened, massing stronger each day. My being slowly shifted from a deep gray to neon green.

As a whole, I felt strong enough to ask a question I had long been harboring in my regrowth. "Have we met before?"

"I wondered when you'd return to the land of the living. Remember me? I'm Selma. Selma Mansion, that is," she said laughing, her old pillars creaking. Her plywood covering empty windowpanes swelled in the wind.

Where was I? Regret pierced my roots. "I don't remember," I said softly, barely more than a whisper. "How did I get here?"

This place seemed familiar, but I didn't know why. Warm sunlight dappled the floors with shadows of tree branches through musty windows. I could almost hear a symphony in the distance and human shoes clacking on wooden floors. But it was silent, save for the birds cawing outside Selma's walls.

"You arrived at the turn of the twentieth century, right before my fire." Selma paused, her old floorboards trembling beneath the weight of the memory. "Then even after they patched me up, you insisted on coming in. They said mosses were always the most resilient plants. I've missed your grit," she said, allowing a sigh of a breeze to travel through her empty rooms.

I remembered the roar of the fire, the crackling beams, and popping glass. I remembered the black, shadowy fading of light through smoke. I remembered my deep slumber as I clung to the minuscule beats of life I had left. I tried to come back for so long. My mat sat dormant for years; the new hole in Selma's roof called me back from those depths.

In the early days before the fire, a long string of families and their friends strode through Selma's rooms. There were winter drafts that seemed to always work their way inside Selma, despite the decades of continuous labor put into her. As the humans went about their lives in jubilance and battles alike, they hardly noticed my existence in their peripheries.

"You remember the kids that always tracked in mud through the doors?" I asked. With mud always came more moss.

"And their laughter that bounced off my walls, echoing up through the spiral stairs?" Selma added. "And there was that one cat that never got the hang of the litter box."

"I wonder what they're doing now," I said.

"Haven't seen them in years. But there are still kids that come to visit, despite the adults trying to keep them out."

"Why would they want to keep them away?" I couldn't imagine this home without children. They grew alongside Selma and me, spreading my spores through their tracks and denting her walls during games with poor attempts at masking them afterward.

"The adults think they'll destroy me. No families live here now. They don't want their art painted on my walls, or their anger expressed through rocks to my windows. There are signs posted telling them to stay away, to keep out. I'm glad they aren't bothered by those. I'm glad to have their life growing within me."

"Everyone needs a place to grow," I said, stretching my shoots, letting the rainwater trickle through me.

***

Something was wrong. Selma was not letting her doors open. With a clang and a thunk, two humans stormed through her front door. She raised dust up around them, entering every possible crevice of their bodies. They sneezed but continued anyway. They weren't children.

I tried to help Selma defend herself by rising my shoots into a shield.

The humans' voices grew loud and abrasive. "There's some vines on the backside of the house, and moss all around the doors in here. You can spray it all and we'll come check on it in a couple weeks."

Moss? Is that what they said? It couldn't be.

The familiar wetness of rain seeped into me, but this felt different. My entire being stung. I shriveled and shrunk, out of control of my own movements. I tried to go deeper into the crack between the baseboard and the wall. I could only move so fast, and not fast enough to stop them. I froze out of fear. Then, when I tried to move, I physically couldn't. They paralyzed me. I recalled those familiar black shadows that surged like fire. The humans walked away as the world faded in front of me.

Selma held me as gently as she could. "I'll see you soon, my friend," she murmured.

I tried to let her know I was still there. A huff of air escaped me, soundless.

***

It seemed as though decades had passed when a splash of water woke me from my slumber. A dog was lapping water from a bowl next to the back door. Satiated, it walked away.

I remembered this place. It felt like home. There was no telling how long I'd been dormant. Despite recognizing my surroundings, I couldn't place where I was.

A gust of wind carried a voice through a sliver in the doorframe. It softly said, "Hey, friend. I've been missing you for ages."

"Have we met before?" I asked, feeling confused. But I was near certain that we had.

Selma, I remembered. She was home.

# Back Road Blues

DEWEY L. YEATTS

Karl and Dutch were hanging out in the break room, winding down from another scorching late-May day working for the Cluster Springs division of the Virginia Department of Transportation, when Will, their supervisor, ambled in, big gut preceding him.

"You seen the weather reports?"

Karl shrugged. His knee hadn't been acting up today. Ever since the a-hole safety from Dan River had hit him low in the knee on a pass breakup, his career as a tight end had been over, and dreams of even a rinky-dink college were gone, leaving him with a limp and dull ache on days when it was crap weather. Not a twinge today. "Nope."

"They're calling for a big one tonight, a cold front smacking into this crazy hot weather we been having, and it's going to be bad. You two are on call tonight."

Dutch cut a look at Karl, Dutch letting his luscious Burt Reynolds' mustache do the talking for him. "Whatever, Will. Long's we get that double-overtime pay."

Dutch needed the money, because alimony was eating him up. Kind of thing that happens to a married guy who had the bad judgement to sleep with his brother's wife. Ever since he hit puberty, the little head had done most of the thinking, hence his nickname. Beat going by his real name, anyway.

"Not going to be bad anyway, Dutch. My knee is more reliable than the weatherman. Count on it."

***

They could barely see the road, the downpour drenched their windshield in waves, like an angry sea.

Dutch was driving, and he didn't dare cut his eyes to Karl. "Your knee, my ass."

When destructive storms raged—high winds, heavy rain, lightning—VDOT rolled crews out in the storm to patrol their territory, looking for downed trees and other road hazards. In the back of the pickup, chainsaws, axes, and the like. They were to clear the road if the tree or branches were manageable for a two-man crew, and report any downed lines, or lines in danger of being downed, to the power company.

Lightning spiked across the sky, lit up the night, but it only made the heavy rain stand out more, like silver in the darkness.

They were about twelve turns off 501, deep in the gosh-darn boonies, where you were lucky if you could peep the state road signs. The roads back here were still paved—they hadn't hit dirt yet. The unlined roads were black and twisting, and it was all Dutch could do to keep the truck on the road.

Then they ran up on a long branch—oak tree, looked like—lying on the road.

Dutch cursed, hit the brakes. Thankfully, the rain began to slack off, and he put on the four-ways, and he and Karl, jackets buttoned tight, slipped on their hard hats and stepped out into the roaring night.

The rain still needled their faces in the relentless wind. The branch was maybe twelve feet long and not too thick, and with a practiced eye, and a year of working together, the men fired up the chainsaw, hacked the limb in two, and dragged the pieces to the gully.

Damn knee was holding up fine, Karl thought.

"What road are we on?" Dutch yelled over the rain and wind.

They needed to mark it, so the cleanup crews tomorrow could cut the limb up more, move it further off the road.

"I thought you knew what road you turned on?"

They threw the saw in the back, climbed in, wiped at the rain on their faces. "I thought you were looking."

Karl leaned back. He peered forward, saw the road ended not too far ahead, the only road connected to it a dirt road, one they didn't need to maintain. "Are we lost, Dutch?"

"Hell, I'm not lost until I'm out of gas and out of cigarettes." He tapped the fuel dial, still over half a tank, and he popped a cigarette out of the pack. "Don't get your panties in a bunch."

Dutch put the truck in gear, did a turn at the dirt road, and headed back the way they came.

This really was the boonies, houses spaced pretty far apart, no businesses other than ones an enterprising sort ran out of their home, and the trees crowded the road. The gullies were chock-full of rain, and the wind was spooling up again.

Dutch hit the stop sign at a T, no houses around, and the lightning lit up the road again.

In front of them, dark forest and the wipers fought the rain pounding down again, and Karl thought he saw something in the woods ahead of them.

The lightning flashed again, and held, three stuttering pulses, and in the strobe of the electricity, Karl watched as a spider the size of a VW Bug lowered itself from the oak trees, blue-white glancing off its myriad dark eyes, and it reached a tentative leg to touch the road in front of the truck.

The stuttering lightning died, and Karl yelled at Dutch to move, and Dutch cranked the wheel to the right, and they fishtailed into the right turn, but Dutch saved it before they hit the gully, white-knuckling the steering wheel, praying the tires caught, and something slammed into the truck bed.

He didn't look back, hit the gas, and kept the truck on the road. In the light of the instruments, his face was white, his mustache drooping around the cigarette he had nearly bitten in two.

An hour later, they were back on a marked road, and the rain had stopped. The wind died down, and they got out of the truck, went to the back. A fist-sized dent buckled the tailgate, and coarse brown hairs, thick as broom straw, were matted into the metal.

At least they did get double overtime pay.

# May 15, 2064

## JAMES BLAKEY

THE SUN ROSE BRIGHT over the Shenandoah Valley, burning off the last wisps of morning mist across New Market Battlefield State Historical Park.

"Ladies and gentlemen, citizens of Earth, and our colonies beyond," a voice echoed from hidden speakers. "Two hundred years ago, a desperate Confederate stand, bolstered by cadets barely out of boyhood, repelled the Union thrust into Virginia's breadbasket amid a drenching rainstorm that turned fields to quagmires. Today, the weather nets guarantee perfect conditions: clear skies and gentle breezes. History, preserved and recreated without its harshest inconveniences."

Holographic banners floated at the field's edges: *The Battle of New Market - Reenacted with 21st-Century Precision.* High above, a swarm of sleek cambots hummed in lazy circles. The fist-sized black spheres with unblinking cyclopean lenses streamed live feeds and augmented-reality overlays across the planet and beyond.

From the south came a low, insistent beat. Drums, the steady, relentless cadence of the long roll. Then a single bugle pierced the morning air: the call to advance, notes rising in urgent summons.

At the tree line, where Breckinridge's men once advanced through pouring rain, the first figures emerged. They moved with eerie fluidity, gray ranks snapping into formation, kepis tilted at regulation angles.

Each rebel stood precisely 179 centimeters tall with shoulders squared beneath unfurled regimental flags. Every step landed with the same measured rhythm on the dewy grass. A faint, almost imperceptible hum carried on the breeze, like the soft whir of a distant engine.

Tesla Optimus-series humanoids, discontinued and obsolete Generation 13-A, repurposed for historical simulation. Their joints whispered with electric servos as they raised replica Enfield rifles.

"For decades, the tradition of Civil War reenactment thrived on human passion, with thousands donning blue and gray, marching through mud and smoke to honor the past. But over time, participation dwindled. The hobby aged out. Younger generations turned to virtual worlds and endless digital distractions.

"In the late 2030s, robots supplemented the few remaining reenactors. Autonomous platforms endured the heat in wool uniforms without complaint, while human volunteers focused on command roles and interpretation.

"By 2053 the shift was complete. The last flesh-and-blood reenactment faded into history. Today, every commemoration, from Gettysburg to Shiloh, is an all-mechanical affair: precise, tireless, and utterly faithful to period tactics."

Another set of drums rolled from the north, then a bugle answered. No wavering pitch, no breathy gaps. Synthetic perfection.

From the rise near Manor's Hill, Federal ranks crested into view, silhouetted against the climbing sun. The Union Boston Dynamics Atlas Mark VII platforms descended in disciplined formation. Renowned for their explosive dynamic mobility in unstructured and chaotic settings, these machines were built on decades of evolution from DARPA-funded prototypes. Their bulkier frames excelled at raw power, rapid whole-body adjustments, and adaptive locomotion—capabilities honed for disaster response, factory work, and accurately recreating the endurance of war-weary troops.

A programmed wind stirred the flags. An AI adjusted the lighting for dramatic effect. The drones tightened their formation, cameras zooming in as the two lines advanced in eerie lockstep, drums thundering a relentless cadence that no human could sustain without faltering.

Robotic crews manning replica Napoleons and Parrotts traded salvos. Muzzles flashed with blank charges, the booms synced to seismic speakers for ground-shaking immersion. Harmless pyrotechnics bloomed overhead.

The Tesla Confederates pushed north across the open field. A bugle signaled, "Fix Bayonets." The blades snapped onto barrels in unison, gleaming as they locked into place.

"Ready... Aim... Fire!" The gray line erupted as one with a devastating volley. Ramrods whipped back in mechanical concert. Smoke generators embedded in their ranks billowed black-powder haze, shrouding the advance in authentic fog as each shot continued, timed to the millisecond.

The next command followed without pause: "Charge bayonets!"

The drones swarmed low, capturing the uncanny ballet: no shouted curses, no wavering lines, only perfect replication of 1864's desperate drill.

"Observe the transition from fire to shock. Volleys to break resolve. Bayonets to seal the rout. The Confederate push mirrors Breckinridge's improvised advance."

Blue ranks answered in layered musketry. Front rank kneeling, second standing, third reloading—attempting to hold the line.

Then the turning point: a programmed gap appeared in the Rebel formation, just as in 1864. A battalion of smaller-framed Optimus Variant 13-Vs surged forward in a flawless charge up the slope toward Bushong's orchard. Their bayonets leveled, strides eating ground without slip, even as the simulated mud from misters and morph-gel terrain pads clung to their boots.

The Confederate pressure proved too much. The Union line buckled under the relentless advance. The Federals began a steady withdrawal north, fire crisp and unerring as the retreat gained momentum.

"The cadets' desperate stand becomes mechanical inevitability. No fear, no hesitation. Only the preservation of valor in unfeeling code."

Atlases fell in waves, systems powering down to mimic death, while the gray ranks pressed on. The remnants of the Union force scrambled over the hill. The Confederates pursued briefly, halting at the programmed boundary.

As the smoke cleared, the field grew silent save for the whir of cooling servos. Flags lowered. Maintenance micro-drones swept the ground, vacuuming spent blanks and retracting terrain pads. Casualties rebooted and rose in unison, their systems running self-diagnostics.

The cambots lingered, lenses panning over empty pavilions and deserted stands. No crowds cheered; no neural links pulsed. Yet the program persisted—year after year, every May 15—for an audience that no longer existed.

# Fish Guts

## S. C. MCCLINTOCK

As she squinted into the rising sun, Miri marveled at the beauty of the Virginia coast, where beams of light streamed over the sea's horizon to paint the clouds with blazes of red and orange.

Then she forced her eyes wide open and sighed as reality smacked her over the head. Norfolk was a blighted, almost abandoned city, where the Atlantic continued moving in without paying rent, the city's skeletal remains jutting up through the water, shedding its crumbling walls as affordable housing for coral and kelp. And today the stench was unforgiving, the rotting algae and fish mixing with everyone's shite from up-river, baked by the oppressive heat and stewed in the ever-present humidity.

Just when the smell couldn't get any worse, Sheril let loose with one of her kelp farts. As Miri's eyes watered, she quipped, "At least put your butt underwater so it will kill us some fish." A few weak laughs drifted through the group. Hard to expect more—their small gang was on edge and starving. Increased patrols had made finding food almost impossible. The same ones who captured Lora last month, which only deepened the group's sullen mood.

Miri winced, remembering her best friend's screams as they hauled her away. And now?

Now we were eight.

Daria shook her head at the smell. "We'll start tonight's hunt with nets in the deeps off the old waterfront, and if that doesn't pan out, we'll head east to the shallows for gigging." Everyone gasped, but Daria was smart enough to head off the obvious, "It's been a year since we've heard a whisper of the Kalupa. We need to focus on food, not imaginary critters."

Miri agreed about the food, but the old locals swore a Kalupa—some child-stealing, flesh-eating sea beast—skulked near the old waterfront and was best left alone.

Daria shrugged off objections. "We paddle in at dusk, keep our eyes open, and we can score some food."

That ended the arguments, fueled by grumbling tummies. But it was risky as hell: the Kalupa might be myth, but open water north of the ruins left them exposed to water-cop drones. Those bastards were starving the locals worse every day—eager to scoop up eight young vagrants and peddle them to work farms or militia as cheap drone bait.

They settled down to let the worst of the day's heat pass, dozing fitfully.

***

Twelve hours later, Miri was paddling her skiff between buildings, scouting ahead in the dying light, fighting the distraction of hunger.

Then she jerked so hard she nearly tipped the skiff as the nasty whine of drone propellers burst through the darkness, echoing off the ruins. She kicked an orange ball off her skiff to warn those behind her while twirling her bola overhead. The drone crept into view, and she nailed it with a perfect throw, sending the wreckage plunging into the black water.

With seconds before the cops rounded the corner, Miri carved a vicious left toward a small gap between buildings, paddling as hard as she could, and saw out of the corner of her eye that Daria and company had turned around. As she knifed between buildings, she took another left into a small alcove, hoping the shadows there would do the rest.

That's when the Kalupa erupted from the water.

Miri almost peed herself. Dark green skin stretched over six long limbs, a hooked beak gaping, with eyes the size of dinner plates staring back. The beast jerked backward, frothing the surface. But then its legs snagged on a submerged floor. It slammed down on its rear, the fish in its grip flying up into the air as it let out a high, panicked scream. Whether from the fall or that little-girl shriek, Miri couldn't help it—she snorted, then burst out laughing.

As the Kalupa struggled to stand, goggles and a mask were strapped to its head—making those dinner-plate eyes look even bigger. And beneath the dark green skin-suit it was clearly wearing clothes. *Actual clothes!*

It fumbled for a button on the mask. A tinny, soft voice crackled: "What is so funny?"

Not a Kalupa. But what?

Boat engines rumbled in the distance. The creature spun toward the sound, ready to bolt.

"Hold it," Miri called. "The cops will search if they spot my boat. Help me sink it?"

The Kalupa didn't hesitate. It spun back and threw its weight onto the skiff's bow, driving the nose under in a rush of water as Miri leapt into the building. She returned hauling rusted furniture. In moments they had the skiff submerged and hidden, then pushed deeper into the ruins.

As she and the creature—who'd introduced himself as "Jak"—traded stories deep into the night, she felt as if she were floating through a dream while he talked about a spaceship crash a hundred years ago, and how he and his crew had survived in the Caribbean. But as the world warmed and tropical fish pushed north, they were forced to follow.

"We need the bacteria from a specific fish's intestines," he said. His crew had built fish farms and oyster beds hidden deep within the submerged structures of Norfolk's ruins, places no skiff could easily reach and where nets snagged on collapsed steel.

"Fish farms? Oyster beds? Like... multiple?" Miri blinked, mental gears whirring. "And you live off fish guts?" Miri's world did not usually engender hope.

*＊＊

But the next morning, as the sun rose over the ocean, she introduced the newest member of their gang. A wee bit of optimism stirred in her soul. Jak was talking to Sheril when she flashed a small grin—and as he gasped, eyes watering.

Miri thought: *Now we were nine.*

# Lifted into the Night

## ELORA KOUNS

SKIING DOWN THE SOFT, fluffy snow-covered hill is what I love most about winter. I breathe in the icy air and settle into the ski lift.

"It's *so* cold up here, Trinity," my friend Sophia says.

I always take her with me on my skiing trips.

"It's perfect skiing weather," I respond.

Sophia sighs, she is obviously starting to regret coming with me. Meanwhile, I am enjoying this trip so much. Fresh ten inches of blower pow blankets the steep mountain. The views of Massanutten are absolutely breathtaking. I could ski up here all day. That is exactly what Sophia and I did.

Several hours later, the slopes are getting ready to shut down. Almost pitch-dark now, the bright, stars are glittering overhead. We race down the smooth hills, powder spraying into my face. I glance over at Sophia, admiring her form even though she looks miserable.

Once we hit the bottom, I start to head back for the lifts.

"Trinity, we don't have time to go again," Sophia explains.

"Don't be such a party-pooper. I have a flow and I only get to come up here so often. I just want to make it worth my time." I plead with my eyes.

"Fine," Sophia agrees.

The attendant is nowhere to be seen. I figure he couldn't have gone far, since the lifts are still running.

"Let's just get on," Sophia says. She's tired and cold, ready to leave now more than ever.

We hop on the still moving lift. The sparkling snow dusting on the tall trees is such an eye catcher. It's all I could stare at until the lift stops.

"What the hell just happened?" Sophia squeals. She cranes her neck, looking wildly in every direction, straining to see what the problem is.

"I'm sure it's nothing. Maybe someone is trying to get on. Ski lifts stop all the time." All I see are the empty chairs ahead and behind.

Sophia is stressing harder, her breathing quick.

"It is going to be OK, Sophia, stop worrying," I assure her.

"How can you say that? We aren't moving at all," Sophia says in a high-pitched, panicking voice.

"Let's just wait. As I said, it could just be someone trying to get on."

We sit there. Seconds turn into minutes. Still no movement. I'm not the type of person to usually worry. But it doesn't take this long to get someone on. But I don't want to show Sophia my fear.

"Do you *still* think it's just someone getting on?" Sophia glares at me with her arms crossed.

I start feeling guilty, because this wouldn't be happening if we had just left.

"Help!" I scream, craning my neck in every direction.

Sophia joins in. We yell for a bit in hopes someone will come. Then, from behind, a deep, rumbling growl rises. It isn't human.

"Thank God!" Sophia exclaims. "Someone is finally coming to save us."

"I don't think that's someone trying to save us." The snarls behind us sound big and heavy. Worries now rush through my head.

We keep pushing each other out of the way, trying to see whatever is making the noise. It sounds like it's getting closer and closer. Then it stops.

"It must be close to us, Trinity," Sophia whispers.

It's so dark and oddly foggy—the fog rolling in suddenly out of nowhere. It's hard to see anything unless it's right up in your face.

Something yanks on the lift. We both gasp.

"Do you feel that, Sophia?" I ask. "Like we're being pulled down?"

"Yeah," Sophia replies, her voice shaking

I twist in the chair, and something catches my eye. It's too far to make out, but it's approaching fast. Soon I can distinguish shapes—a figure climbing the cable.

"What is that?" I ask.

"What is *what?*" Sophia replies.

As it drew closer, the figure came into focus. It was a person... but without a face. No eyes, no nose, no mouth. Completely blank. And it was coming straight for us.

We start screaming, "Help! Help us!"

The figure—it's a man—is coming in fast. I cover my face, praying this is a dream. After a heartbeat, I peek through my fingers. He's gone. Vanished. Maybe it really is just a dream.

"Is he—*it* gone?" Sophia asks in a panicked voice.

"Looks like it." I sigh in relief.

*BAM!* He's suddenly standing on the chair in front of us, only a few feet away. We scream. He tilts his head and lets out a deafening screech. We fall silent. He lurches forward, struggling to rise. He looks weak, in pain. Then gigantic feathery wings burst from his back. The screeching stops.

We stare at him while he kneels there. Nothing happens.

"Who are you? What do you want?" I ask.

The man tilts his blank head up toward us. Sophia and I sit frozen in silence. If he has no eyes or ears, maybe staying quiet means he can't hear us.

He cocks his head to the side. Then he lunges. Grabs us and hauls us into the air.

***

We were *never* seen again.

# Broad Street Station

## JENNIFER BELOTE

ART'S CLAIM TO FAME is that he once met Elvis Presley.

It happened the same day he was offered the position of Earth Ambassador to X-952b.

He walked into Broad Street Station on June 30, 1956, heading to his interview, and held the door for the man coming out. When he pulled the heavy thing open and saw who it was, he froze, eyes wide, jaw hanging open like he forgot how it worked.

"I held the door for him," Art would say, "and he said, 'Thank you, thank you very much.'"

His wife, Irene, heard that story so many times she could recite it word for word. She never understood what the big deal was, considering what her husband had done for a living their entire marriage.

She was meant to have believed he was a building porter at the train station. She discovered the truth by accident when Art forgot his lunch and she took two bus transfers to make sure he didn't go hungry that day.

Irene was only twenty-two years old, inexperienced and barely knew the city. It was a Friday, an unusually cold day for October in Richmond. The station was packed when she arrived: men in suits moving like they had important deadlines, women in curved hats and A-line wool coats strolling through the concourse as if they lived on a different planet than Irene. She wished she were more like them—elegant, sure of herself—and wanted more from life than bus rides and making sure her husband ate.

This having been her first visit to Broad Street Station, she stopped at the information desk.

"Hello," she said, voice small. "My name is Irene. My husband, Art, forgot his lunch this morning, and I was wondering if you could keep it for him?"

"You could take it to him yourself, ma'am," the clerk replied. "You'll want to take the utility wing. Down those stairs and to the right. His room is the second door on the left. He could be anywhere in the station fixing a light bulb, but you can wait for him if you'd like."

She thanked him and followed the directions, heart in her throat as she weaved through people hurrying through the station. She knocked on the big steel door. No answer. Then she pushed it open a few inches, struggling with its weight, and peeked inside.

"Art? It's me, Irene. You forgot your lunch."

Still nothing.

She pushed the door wider. The room was tiny, lit by a single bare bulb on a pull chain that looked too bright for the space. A square analog clock hung lopsided on the wall. The only furniture was a metal chair with no cushion.

She hadn't expected windows, but she'd believed he at least had a desk. She knew he spent most of his time roaming the station, but this was absurd. The indignity of it made her cheeks hot. She sat down on the metal chair, Art's lunch in her lap, and decided she would wait. When he came back, she'd try to talk him into finding better work.

She hadn't been sitting long when the wall in front of her flashed into a swirl of purple and green, like someone had melted a stained-glass window. She stiffened. Not breathing, not blinking, just fused to the chair.

Then from the shimmering mess, a head popped out.

"Irene?" it said. "What are you doing here?"

That was the last thing she remembered before the floor crashed into her head.

When she came to, the colors were gone, and Art was kneeling beside her, patting her cheeks and calling her name.

She sat up, Art's hand on her back to steady her.

"The wall," she whispered. "It was... on."

Art exhaled as if he'd been holding the truth in his chest for years. He helped Irene to the chair.

"Darling, I promised I'd never lie to you. The truth is—I'm not really a building porter. I'm an ambassador. For Earth. That thing you saw was the portal I use to go to my real job."

A high ringing drowned everything out. Irene pinched her arm. It hurt. This was real.

Art rubbed the back of his neck. "You were never supposed to find out. What are you doing here?"

Irene blinked and remembered his pastrami sandwich. She scanned the room, found the silver lunchbox on the floor, and held it up.

"You forgot your lunch," she managed.

"Oh, honey." He kissed her cheek. "You're too good to me."

Then his eyes lit up, bright. "Say! How about I take you out to lunch instead?"

It was such a normal question that Irene grabbed onto it as a tether to reality.

"Where?" she asked, still dazed.

Art grinned, pulled something from his pocket and aimed it at the wall. The gray slab came alive once more.

"Someplace special," he said.

He held out his hand. She looked up at his smiling face, knowing she was safe with him, then held out hers. Together, they stepped through to X-952b.

After the station closed in 1975 and turned into a Science Museum, Art kept his same job, same keys, and same portal. Only the travelers were swapped for tourists.

Later, whenever Betty from across the street tried to brag about her one trip to Niagara Falls, Irene just smiled. She'd walked under two moons and had a favorite café overlooking a red ocean. Niagara didn't impress her much.

And she's always let Art tell the story about Elvis, knowing it is his favorite memory of Earth. Sometimes, when Irene brings his lunch, she finds him in the hall outside the gift shop staring at the photo of the singer walking out of Broad Street Station.

# The Luray Lantern

## KHAYELIHLE

IN THE HEART OF the Shenandoah Valley, nestled between the blue-grey humps of the Blue Ridge Mountains and the whispering caverns of Luray, stood a weathered general store, suspended in the hush of the Civil War. The paint peeled in long, curling strips, like memories the building refused to shed. Locals called it Miss Addie's, though no one alive had actually seen Miss Addie in more than forty years. And yet, the store was always open. Always stocked, always waiting.

Except on the night of the lantern.

Every year on the winter solstice, when the sky was its darkest, and the mountains breathed frost, a single lantern appeared in the store's front window. No one ever saw who placed it there. It simply manifested a soft green glow pulsing like a heartbeat inside a ribcage of dusty glass.

And every year someone disappeared.

This year, that someone was Elijah Boone.

Elijah was a junior park ranger, six months into his assignment patrolling the Luray Caverns and the surrounding forest. He was bright, earnest, a lover of maps and moss and rocks. He heard the stories about Miss Addie's lantern—how it lured the lonely, curious, broken. But Elijah didn't believe in ghost tales. He believed in soil samples, in what he could measure.

So when the green glow flickering through the trees on the night of December 21st, he told himself it was probably a reflection or prank.

Still, he followed it.

Branches snagged at his jacket as if trying to drag him back. The cold felt too sharp like it was watching. When he finally stepped out of the treeline, the general store came into view leaning slightly to the left, as though exhausted by the burden of so many years. Its porch sagged, windows smudged with dust, yet the lantern glowed steadily behind the glass. Shadows danced as if warming their hands at a fire only they could feel.

Elijah swallowed hard and pushed open the creaking door. The bell above the frame hung motionless, as if it had forgotten how to jingle. The air smelled of cedar and cinnamon, an aroma that wrapped around him like an embrace he didn't remember asking for. Shelves lined with goods too old to belong. Tins of hardtack, jars of molasses, hand-stitched quilts, yet everything stood in perfect order, untouched by dust or decay.

Behind the counter stood a woman in a calico dress, her hair pinned in a style that hadn't been fashionable since Reconstruction. Her skin glowed faintly, like something illuminated from within. Her eyes shimmered like mica, holding depths that made Elijah's stomach twist.

"Evening, Ranger Boone," she said softly.

He froze. "How do you know my name?"

Her smile unfolded slowly, like something practiced. "The lantern only calls those it's chosen."

A cold sensation crawled up his back. "Chosen for what?"

She didn't answer with words at first. Instead, she gestured to a wooden box on the counter. Its surface was carved with runes that seemed to shift when he tried to focus on them, writhing like living script.

"Virginia remembers," she murmured. "Land, blood, and stories. Every year, it chooses a Keeper. Someone to carry the lantern and walk the forgotten paths."

A nervous laugh escaped him. "Is this some kind of reenactment? Because if it is, this is quite the production."

Her smile died. "You think this is some kind of game?" she said, voice suddenly brittle. "The lantern holds the memory of every soul lost to this land—soldiers, settlers, slaves, wanderers. Without a Keeper, they drift. They forget themselves. And when they forget..." Her eyes darkened. "They hunger."

The lantern in the box flared green to gold, bright enough to cast trembling shadows across the walls.

Elijah stumbled back. "No. No, I'm not part of this. I didn't sign up for whatever this is."

"No one does," she said gently. "But the land has chosen."

The box creaked open on its own. Inside, the lantern glowed gold now, warm and ancient. A gentle heat brushed Elijah's face, then deepened, curling into his bones like a memory not his own. His breath shuddered. His vision trembled. A pressure grew behind his eyes, as though something was waiting to be let in.

"Take it," the woman whispered.

His hand rose without his permission.

The moment his fingers closed around the lantern's handle, a burst of light swallowed him whole.

***

Elijah awoke standing on a high ridge overlooking the silver-black ribbon of the Shenandoah River. The lantern hung from his belt now, glowing gold, its light casting elongated shadows that whispered in languages he didn't know yet somehow understood.

He began to walk.

Through forests where the trees bent toward him, leaves rustling in greeting. Through battlefields where spectral drums beat faintly, as if echoing from centuries away. Through abandoned towns that flickered between centuries one moment modern, the next lit by oil lamps.

He met others.

A woman in a Confederate uniform, her hands trembling as she searched the fields for the lover she lost. A Tuscarora boy who sang to the stars, his voice trembling with centuries of displacement. A jazz pianist who played for no audience, his music drifting like smoke.

Each time he encountered one, the lantern glowed brighter. Each time, a story sank into his bones heavy, beautiful and unbearable.

Elijah realized, with a hollow ache, that he was no longer alone inside his own skin.

He was the Keeper now.

***

Back in the waking world, Miss Addie's store stood empty again. No lantern in the window. No footprints in the frost.

Locals shook their heads, muttered about another lost soul, and warned their children to stay away. But on misty mornings, hikers on the Appalachian Trail reported seeing a strange figure in a ranger's uniform, walking with a golden lantern that sang like cicadas and smelled of cedar and cinnamon.

# Chessie's Fiddler

## Tara Eckenroad

THE SHIP DRIFTED LISTLESSLY in the calm of the bay near Williamsburg. The stench of unwashed bodies filled the prison ship, the small portal windows barely delivering any air to the Colonials trapped inside. The door burst open and a young man clad in the distinctive red pants, stiffened powdered hair and high collar of the enemy was flung in, landing with a concerning thud. A fiddle followed, landing with a hollow clang. Bloodied and battered, he mumbled in a strange language as he struggled to crawl toward the fiddle, eyes nearly swollen shut, legs dragging heavily behind him.

A Scottish prisoner warily approached, frowning. He recognized the Irish lilt in the man's pained speech.

"Is that Gaelic?" another captive asked.

"Aye. But Irish, I think," the first prisoner replied.

The captured doctor, compelled to examine even an enemy, came closer as the prisoners sought to understand the wheezed garble from the battered Irishman, blood dripping between his cracked teeth.

"Broken back, caved ribs and more minor wounds." The doctor hung his head, the tortured, shameful death sentence rendered by his diagnosis evident even to the laymen present.

"Conscripted. Tried to run to us so they beat 'im an' gave 'im 'is wish," the Scotsman added in a hushed whisper.

The prisoners carried the shattered wretch across the hold and cradled him in a hammock strung near the open porthole, his fiddle resting on his chest.

***

The next day the Irishman had stirred slightly, feverishly strumming half-melodies the men could piece together. The broken fragments of songs created a welcome distraction, and they settled into taking turns to care for the enemy soldier.

As evening descended, the water began to swirl as the songs reached more than man's ears. Several prisoners taking turns at the portholes spied a creature in the water. Perceiving that the great eyes rising from the darkening waters were indeed real, the men gasped; others shoved them aside as they staggered back, their skin pallid in the dim candlelight.

The large sea serpent cocked her head, curious at the melodies.

Cannonballs pelted her hide like angry gnats as the British guards fired vainly to deter her. Dull thuds and shrill shrieks of terror broke across the beautiful serenade.

With a loud whip of her tail, she sent debris and men flying as the ship erupted in a hailstorm of splinters—still eagerly peering through the burning havoc for the source of her joy.

For a brief moment hope filled the prisoners below, replaced with horror and agony as their avenue of freedom was blocked by smoke and clogged by bodies and flotsam. As men and splintered wood collided midair, the thunderous crashes and surging waves masked her approach, letting her glide unseen toward her fiddler.

The enemy soldier found himself adrift on a board, clutching his beloved fiddle. Drunk on pain, he tried to swim, a vague awareness of his own kicking stabbing through the mental fog. Hands grasped his sopping shirt, yanking him from the bloody, ashy water onto a chunk of mast just as the waves reduced the wreck to smoldering driftwood.

The creature's short snorts and huffs sent shivers racing from the survivors' spines to their chattering teeth. Weakly coaxing wet music from the dripping fiddle once more, the Irishman gulped for breath as he watched the beast draw closer—a cheerful gleam in her eyes while fear widened his own. Carefully swimming beneath the debris, she carried the mast to shore, wiggling about to the renewed music and slowing to a creep to savor the soft, trembling notes—unfazed by the other prisoners climbing aboard as she did.

Timidly, the fiddler stumbled closer to her, playing reels and ballads, growing oblivious to the others dashing into the woods behind him—their voices robbed by fear. She splashed about in the shallows, chirping along with her eyes closed, drawing nearer to nuzzle her musician.

He reached out, touching her water-smoothed scales, and smiled as he scratched her chin like a favored pet. "Thanks, luv," he whispered, tears in his eyes.

Enjoying the caresses as much as the music, she lowered her head in invitation. Grateful, he eased onto her broad head, wincing at the strain, the cold sea-night air a welcome relief as they rode back out to sea.

After a few minutes, a white, misty ship gliding effortlessly through the choppy, debris-strewn water came into focus. Every instinct of logic and terror screamed warnings he blithely ignored, too absorbed in cherishing the miraculous return of feeling to his legs—his smile widening in the drifting sea breeze. The beast lifted her head to show him: the ghostly ship was already crewed.

"Chessie. Lass, no. Ye be knowin' better than to bring the livin' back," one of the spirits gently scolded.

"Related to Nessie, are ye, luv?" the musician asked, patting her head.

The ghost offered a hand out of habit. "Occasionally she keeps a living one," he said.

"Normally she finds us floating along the bottom in our grave wraps, works us free, and carries us off to Davy Jones's locker." He spoke as the fiddler waited atop Chessie's head.

She floated alongside the ship until dawn neared, then with a gentle turn lowered her head and deposited the fiddler onto the deck. To his astonishment, the wood felt solid beneath his feet; the crew's hands instinctively reached out to steady him, and—miraculously—he felt no pain in his ribs.

"Sorry lad. Welcome aboard Chessie's crew."

"Wait...?"

"Aye lad. Not sure how or when, but ye're one of us now. Sailing about doing as she invites us along to shuttle souls to the Locker, fight the pirates trying to steal oysters, or anyone out to hurt the creatures she shares these waters with. Less you want to stay in the Locker."

Chessie studied him, her great eyes soft and expectant.

He felt his head nod. "Alright luv. I'll be ye fiddle man."

# Sovereign Battlestate Virginia

## MATTHEW J. TURNER

IN THE FINAL YEARS of the Anno Domini era, mankind had driven its planet to the breaking point. The combined weight of humanity's unchecked avarice and capacity for violence proved too much to bear. Both figuratively and literally, the combined wars exacted their heavy toll, and the Earth cracked and was ripped asunder, the oceans boiling and the continents splitting.

But this is not that story. This is a story of mankind departing the shattered cradle of its birth, leaving the era of God behind for the Post-Earth age, and the mysteries and dangers of the universe that follow. A story of a spacefaring state that disembarked from its home planet but kept its native soil, a landmass given new life aboard the alloyed hull of a hypercarrier. Exactly 42,775 square miles of earth, forest and mountain, towns and cities, humans and wildlife, all lay wrapped in powerful binding fields and armed with devastating weapons to safeguard its people adrift in the sea of stars.

This is the story of the *Sovereign Battlestate Virginia*.

"You'll tear the state apart!" Commander Davis Pendleton cried out as the bridge lurched from the sudden acceleration. The ship containing the entire state of Virginia went into a sickening bank as it raced around the gravity slingshot of the supermassive gas giant Kappa Andromedae b. Streaks of bending light from alien energy weapons tore past the battlestate, vaporizing one of the dozens of moons orbiting this inhospitable planet, as the Kalaghan cruiser gave hot pursuit to *Virginia*.

"She's the Old Dominion, she can take it!" Captain Sterling Van Holloway slapped the arm of his command chair, a confident grin on his face, his voice full of braggadocio. While the rest of the crew groaned under the crushing g-forces, pinned to their seats, Van Holloway was leaning forward, his eyes locked onto the forward viewscreen. The state's computer tracked the hundreds of chunks of melted nickel and iron that used to be cores as the ship bobbed and weaved through the increasingly perilous debris belt that ringed the planet.

"Captain, we have to pull out and slow down!" Pendleton slurred.

Beside him, an orderly bent over and hurled into a sick bag.

"Nuts to the Ninth Nebula, I say to that!" Van Holloway waved off his subordinate's concerns. "If you don't have the chest hair for the job, then let me show you how a real man romances a lady!"

Van Holloway hammered a series of buttons on the arm of his chair. A yoke emerged from the console in front of him, as the viewscreen flashed: **CAPTAIN'S MANUAL OVERRIDE CONFIRMED.**

"Hello, sweet darling," Van Holloway purred as his fingers wrapped around the twin sticks like they were the shoulders of a lover—if said lover was in fact a 375-trillion-ton landmass atop twenty nuclear pulse engines. He fed more power to said engines, pushing the battlestate even faster as it, boosted by the gravity well, approached 0.5% of light speed, nearly 3.5 million miles per hour. Sirens blared in every home, town, and settlement, warning residents to strap themselves in and seek shelter. *Virginia* creaked and groaned from the extreme stress, but Van Holloway smirked and whispered sweet nothings into her ears as the vessel blazed around the orbit of Kappa. Asteroids skimmed off the defensive fields and armor plating, causing the entire state to jostle and shake like a possessed girl shown a Jefferson Bible.

"Oh, mama! She's got the curves of Texas, but the speed of Indiana!" Van Holloway hooted as he struggled to keep on the slingshot path.

A tremendous crash nearly threw Van Holloway out of his seat. The lights flickered, then dimmed. Red emergency strips flashed on as the forward display blazed with cascading warnings.

Lieutenant Thomas Orrery struggled out of his chair to take stock of the damage. "Impact, impact! Hole in the atmosphere field above Richmond!"

On the tenth aft viewscreen, clouds were venting into cold space. A Kalaghan photoid had finally made contact, the overlapping defensive fields barely preventing a catastrophic atmospheric loss, but the damage was done.

"Tell them to hold their breath!" Van Holloway shouted back.

"Landslide down the Appalachians into the Shenandoah!" Lieutenant Genevieve Gennaro cried out.

"They've got shovels, they'll be fine!" Van Holloway waved her off. They'd almost made it around the planet when a transmission flashed on the screen.

"Ho there, *Virginia!* Looks like you could use a hand from the ol' Buckeye!" A gravelly voice boomed as a uniformed man with a heavy five o'clock shadow waved the main monitor. Captain Odysseus Grant.

"It's *Ohio!*" Pendleton cheered. "Ohio's here and charging weapons!"

"Ugh. Of course it's *Ohio,*" Van Holloway rolled his eyes. Even after Earth exploded, he *still* couldn't get away from blasted *Ohio.* "Well, don't let it be said that Virginia looks gift horses in the mouth. Maintain speed, all power to guns!"

"Sir? We aren't leaving?" Pendleton asked.

"Did George Washington leave when the British burned down the White House in 1812?" Van Holloway asked.

"Um, no, that was—"

"Exactly, Commander! Now, wait for my mark! We aren't going to let *Ohio* take all the credit for this battle!"

As soon as *Virginia* whipped around the gas giant, she lined up a clear shot on the Kalaghan cruiser, Ohio gleaming in the distance like an uninvited guest at a duel. The twin states opened fire, hundreds of mass drivers slinging thousands of tons of kinetic force across the void of space. Massive kinetic slugs ripped through the Kalaghan cruiser. She erupted in star-spangled fireworks, enough to bring a tear to Van Holloway's eye and a hand to his heart.

"God bless America, and God bless sweet Virginia."

# About the Authors

**Grace Athanasiou — One for the Mountain Folk**

Grace Athanasiou is a speculative fiction author. Her short stories have been featured in several magazines and anthologies. Her story "Beautiful Monster" was recommended by editor Ellen Datlow for *The Best Horror of the Year Volume Sixteen.* She lives in New York City.

web: chillsubs.com/profile/graceathanasiou

**Madeline Barnicle — Theophany on the Stockton**

Madeline Barnicle received a PhD in mathematical logic from UCLA, and now lives in Maryland. Like the finely-dressed woman on the Staples Mill mural, she loves to see Richmond by rail!

web: madeline-barnicle.neocities.org

**Robin E. Bates — The Reeds of Percival's Island**

Robin E. Bates is an English professor at the University of Lynchburg who made Virginia her home in 2008. She will never tire of the mystic beauty of the Blue Ridge and the foothills.

web: lynchburg.edu/robin-bates
li: Robin E. Bates
th: @britlitgirl
tt: @robinbates6

### Jennifer Belote — Broad Street Station

Jennifer Belote is a writer/illustrator living in Richmond, Virginia. Her idea of a perfect day is drowning out the world with noise-canceling headphones and letting her coffee go cold as she brings alternate realities to life for children and adults.

 web: behance.net/jenniferbee

### Sarah Benton — 2609 West Grace Street

Sarah Benton is a Virginia native, currently working as a software engineer in Richmond. She received Highest Honors in the Writer's College 2025 Short Story Competition, and she has published poetry with IHRAM Press. Her dream is to soon publish a novel.

### James Blakey — May 15, 2064

James is the author of *Superstition*, a paranormal thriller and two short story collections, *The Cat Who Loved David Duchovny* and *Fast Times at Spiro Agnew High.* He lives in Broadway

 web: jamesblakeywrites.com
 ig: @jamesblakeyauthor
 x: @jameswblakey

### Caitlyn Brooke — The Trees

Caitlyn Brooke is a speculative fiction writer living in Arlington, VA. Her work melds the absurdities of modern life with the fantastical, revealing that reality is often the strangest thing of all. Though she has been writing for over a decade, this is her first submission intended for publication.

 web: tumblr.com/cb-author

## Ember Brooks — Hope is a Thing with Brittle Scales

Ember is a Writer/Editor who calls the Shenandoah Valley home, along with her husband and two cats. She holds two degrees in writing and spent six years working with National Parks. She can now be found in her home office surrounded by green things, books, and half-finished hobby projects.
web: ember.ink
ig: @emberbrooks.books

## Jessica Carboni — Blue Haze

Jessica Carboni is a Canadian writer raised in Montreal, QC. She holds a Bachelor of Arts from McGill University with a concentration in English Literature, Art History, and Classics.

## Adam S. Crowe — Mother of Presidents

Adam S. Crowe is the author of *Henry Sinclair and the Dream Riders* and the upcoming *Henry Sinclair and the T-Shirt of Destiny*. He writes fun, imaginative, and adventurous stories (mostly) for kids that are a love letter to stories he experienced as a child.
fb: facebook.com/adamcrowewrites
ig: @adamcrowewrites
link: linktr.ee/adamcrowewrites

## Alexis Collins — The Bakery by Campus

Alexis Collins earned her BA in English, Creative Writing from Randolph College and her MFA in Creative Writing from Hollins University. Her work has appeared in *Flash Fiction Magazine*. She's from the Richmond metro area of Virginia and works in marketing.
th: @lexiscee17

### r.a.t. dubrueler — Late for Muster

A proud West Virginian, Rachel Ann Taylor DuBrueler grew up loving dark, twisty stories, with a knack for spotting the killer before the credits rolled. A corporate strategist by day, she's completed five novels designed to linger long after the last page, and she lives in Richmond with her husband and rescued Dobermans, who only pretend to guard the property.

    web: rachelthewriter.com
    fb: facebook.com/profile.php?id=61578899596179
    x: @ratdubrueler

### Tara Eckenroad — Chessie's Fiddler

Tara Eckenroad is from Blairsville, Pennsylvania and has lived in Harrisonburg for almost 19 years. Her primary hobby when not writing is historical dance presentation and performing voluntary chaplaincy.

### Arlen Fain — An Encounter in the Great Dismal Swamp

Arlen Fain was born and raised in East Texas, spending his early years between Trinity and Cherokee counties. He studied literature at the University of Texas and now lives in Virginia, with his wife, Everleigh Rose, and their four children. Fain writes horror, weird fiction, fantasy, sci-fi, and poetry that considers the gritty and atmospheric aspects of life.

    fb: facebook.com/p/Arlen-Fain-61576222906161
    ig: @arlen_fain

### MaryJune Haines — Trail Magic

MaryJune is a writer living in the Shenandoah Valley. She studied screenwriting before pivoting to prose as her dreams of making it as a filmmaker died and flowers bloomed over their tombstones. She has two cats.

    ig: @maryjunewrites

## David Horn — Run the Ridges & Sirens of the Chesapeake

David Horn is a speculative fiction writer whose work has appeared or will appear in *Analog Science Fiction and Fact* and others. He lives in Colorado.
    amzn: amazon.com/stores/David-Horn/author/B0F8DZZ52B
    bs: @dave0258.bsky.social
    fb: facebook.com/horndw

## Kurt Johnson — Back of the Dragon

Kurt Johnson is a career higher education administrator. His fiction writing craft has evolved from years of creating humorous rhymes for friends and family. Now, he yearns to share more broadly his work in historical and fantasy fiction. He lives in the beautiful Shenandoah Valley of Virginia.

## Khayelihle — The Luray Lantern

Khayelihle Benghu resides in Johannesburg, South Africa. Besides writing she has a heart for photography mainly nature.
    ig: @khayelihlebenghu

## Elora Kouns — Lifted into the Night

Elora Kouns is a student at Spotswood High School. She is originally from the Richmond, Virginia area, and moved to Harrisonburg. She will graduate in 2026 and has plans on going to college. She loves to do art, and hopes to pursue a career in writing.
    ig: @elora.kouns

**Carol Parris Krauss — Luellen with the Emerald Shoes**

Ms. Parris Krauss is honored to have published in *Louisiana Lit*, the *Arkansas Review, Salvation South, Story South, The South Carolina Review*, and the *Mid/South Sonnet Anthology*. Fernwood Press published her full-length book *Mountain.Memory. Marsh.* in November of 2025. She currently lives in Virginia with her St. Bernard, Martha June.
   web: carolparriskrausspoet.org
   fb: facebook.com/carolpkrauss
   ig: @carolpkrauss

**Merit La Frenière — Commonwealth of Crows & Mrs. Hensley's Home for Well-Behaved Spirits**

Merit La Frenière is a writer and ninth-generation Virginian with a deep love of language, strange tales, and cats. When she isn't wandering local graveyards in search of ancestors, she can be found browsing the aisles of bookstores or writing her next story in a noisy café. She lives near Harrisonburg.

**Jane Limprecht — The General's Gold**

Jane Limprecht's short stories have appeared or are forthcoming in four crime fiction anthologies and *Kings River Life Magazine*. She lives in Springfield, walks along the wooded trail to Lake Accotink, and commuted on the VRE before she retired.
   web: janelimprecht.wordpress.com

## Jeannie Marschall — Manifest

Jeannie Marschall (she/her/any) is a European garden hag who reads, writes, and forages as much as possible. The results can be found in various pantries & bookcases, thanks to e.g. *Flash Fiction Online, Snowflake Mag*, Tenebrous Press, or Black Spot Books. Longer works—predominantly folklore-themed & queer—are simmering in the cauldron (ETA 2026).

bs: @jeanniemarschall.bsky.social

## Megan McClintock — In Bad Faith & The Called the Body Jane

Megan McClintock is a writer of speculative and supernatural fiction. She lives with her cat at the edge of a wood in Charlottesville. She holds a B.A. in Anthropology and International Relations from the University of Virginia.

## S. C. McClintock — Fish Guts

Sam McClintock is an environmental scientist and cyber consultant living in Williamsburg. He has worked with the EPA, industry and government contractors, served with the Army Rangers and Defense Intelligence Agency, and his alma mater is NCSU.

## Carey Ann Miller — Finding Sea Glass

Carey Ann Miller lives in Richmond with her husband and works as an attorney. She writes in her free time, and she also loves to hike, golf, spend time with her family, and visit the Eastern Shore of Virginia.

## Jon Negroni — Please Remain on the Marked Path

Jon Negroni is a Puerto Rican author based in California. His most recent fiction has been published with IHRAM Press, *The Fairy Tale Magazine*, and *Speculation Publications*. Jon was a finalist for the 2025 BCLF Elizabeth Caribbean-American Writer's Prize and is a *Best American Short Stories of 2025*-nominated writer.

    web: jonnegroni.com
    bs: @jonnegroni
    ig: @jonnegroni

## Kent M. Peterson — Ghost Story

Kent M. Peterson has lived in Virginia most of his life. He worked for many years as a software tester, but now focuses on gardening and writing.

    web: kaempii.wordpress.com
    x: @bykentmpeterson

## Steve Porter — Lights in the Lake

Steve Porter came from a small town in central Virginia and grew up with a love of storytelling and mystery. He channeled that love into a passion for writing and crafting fantastical worlds, with hopes to publish the stories rattling around in his head, from supernatural thrillers to space operas.

    ig: @redrangersteve

**Jen Poteet — Move to the Country, They Said. It Will be Relaxing, They Said...**

Jen Poteet dwells in the foothills of the Blue Ridge Mountains with her family and a menagerie of pets. When she isn't writing or making art you can find her at Black Sheep Studios the tattoo studio she owns with her husband. She has four published works and has published short stories in several anthologies and online journals.

fb: facebook.com/jenpoteet
ig: @jenpoteet

**Stephen A. Roddewig — Tour Unit 73Y**

Stephen A. Roddewig is an author residing in Arlington. Born in Leesburg, he grew up hiking in the Blue Ridge Mountains and made many trips to visit his grandparents and cousins in Virginia Beach. He attended James Madison University and has toured almost every cavern in the Shenandoah Valley.

web: stephenaroddewig.com
ig: @stephen.drinks.for.his.book

**Arre Shane — Rebirth**

Arre Shane is a scientist and college professor in western Virginia. He writes fiction and science fiction short stories.

**Carol Steele — Listen to Miss Nellie**

Carol writes about events she hopes will never happen; her genres are mystery and psychological horror. An avid reader, history and biographies are her main focus, and she prefers fiction that doesn't end tied in a neat little bow. Her writing leaves room for readers' imaginations to further the story.

email: carolsteelewrites@yahoo.com

## Griff Thomas — Rubilacxe

Cinematic, irreverent, funny, evocative, and unexpected heroes color Griff's work. Short stories "Rubilacxe" and "The Whitetail Whatchamacallit" appear in the Fantastic Anthologies. Upmarket fiction novels *Breaking the Surface* and *Killing the Corporation* are available to publishers. Ten plays, thirty short stories, one rock opera, and *Eldrij Parq* alternative albums showcase his creative range.

web: griffthomasauthor.net

## Alex Tucker — Leave No Trace

Alex Tucker is an HWA writer from Virginia. His novella *Afraid to Feel* recently debuted through Alien Buddha Press, and two more books will publish in 2026/2027. Alex's short fiction has been featured in *Occupying Bodies* from Black Hare Press, *Carols for the Dead* from Desiree Horton, and *Creepy Podcast.*

ig: @alextuckerwrites
link: linktr.ee/alextuckerwrites
th: @alextuckerwrites

## Matthew J. Turner — Sovereign Battlestate Virginia

Matthew is a U.S. history teacher and artist who lives in Winchester with his beautiful wife and their sweet little cat. He especially enjoys both studying and writing about World War II and the Cold War, and as a reader and author enjoys science fiction and fantasy. He was previously published in the *Shenandoah Fantastic* collection.

fb: facebook.com/matthew.turner.376
ig: @matthewturnerart

**Shannon Wagoner — The Grit in the Baseboards**

Shannon Wagoner lives in Charlottesville with their wife and their four-legged creatures. When they're not writing they work with infants and toddlers, and enjoys cloud-watching and macro film photography.

ig: @shanwagoner

**Dewey L. Yeatts — Back Road Blues**

Dewey L. Yeatts lives in Pennsylvania now, but was born and raised in Halifax County, Virginia, and worked two summers for VDOT. He is married, and has had stories published by Three Ravens and Hellbound Books, among others.

# Other Fantastic Anthologies

A Vampire at a UVA Sorority...

A 400-year-old Dragon Hidden in Shenandoah National Park...

An Enigmatic Tuxedo Cat on the Downtown Mall...

These are just a few of the characters you will encounter in ***CHARLOTTESVILLE FANTASTIC: ARCANE ECHOES FROM VIRGINIA'S HEARTLAND.***

Twenty tales in total, each exploring the mystical essence of the region, revealing a place where the past, present, and future intertwine in unexpected and enchanting ways.

Some funny, some serious, all just a little spooky, there really is something in this collection for everyone. Whether you are a born and bred Charlottesvillian or a visitor looking for a book to give you a feel for the local culture, ***CHARLOTTESVILLE FANTASTIC*** is bound to capture your attention and spark your imagination. —**Samantha Koon Jones**, Book Critic for *The (Charlottesville) Daily Progress*

***CHARLOTTESVILLE FANTASTIC*** in eBook, paperback, and hardcover from your favorite book retailer.

# Other Fantastic Anthologies

Time travelers at the Shakespeare Center...

Trolls beneath Luray Caverns...

A ghost train in Woodstock...

Meet them in ***SHENANDOAH FANTASTIC: ARCANE ECHOES FROM VIRGINIA'S VALLEY***.

Twenty-four speculative tales that reveal the uncanny spirit of the Valley—a place where folklore breathes, history whispers, and the extraordinary waits just beyond the next ridge.

> The twenty-four stories in ***SHENANDOAH FANTASTIC*** invite readers to see the Shenandoah Valley not just as a beautiful and historic landscape, but as a living repository of mystery and magic. These extraordinary tales, rooted in the Valley's famously fertile soil, sprout new and enthralling dimensions of reality that will forever alter your view of this region.
> —**Chris Bolgiano, Author of *The Appalachian Forest***

***SHENANDOAH FANTASTIC*** in eBook, paperback, and hardcover from your favorite book retailer.

# From Whitaker Lyon Press

# THE CAT WHO LOVED DAVID DUCHOVNY

From the pen of Derringer Award-winning author James Blakey comes three fantastical tales.

**THE CAT WHO LOVED DAVID DUCHOVNY**

Madame Marie Curie, a Blue Point Siamese, spends her days binge-watching episodes of *The X-Files*. When Marie's owner Jim invites Debbie—the new girl from work—over for dinner, Marie resigns herself to a night of sulking while watching the couple with disdain. But Debbie has set her sights on something more than a free meal, and it will take all of Marie's feline cunning to stop her.

**THE WITCH OF SHERMAN OAKS**

Jennifer Griffiths, the self-styled Witch of Sherman Oaks, is part life coach, part therapist. Her week isn't going well. The rent is due, and the big-time reality star that Jennifer was counting on as new client just walked out. When the oddly dressed Braxtiaran Darahenij hires Jennifer to do some roleplaying and face off against an evil sorcerer at some junior league Burning Man, she jumps at the chance. Sure LARPers are odd, but Brax is paying with real gold. But the sorcerer isn't playing. He has the power to destroy the Earth. Now it's up to The Witch of Sherman Oaks to stop him.

**THE LAST MISSION**

John Linn's latest assignment seems simple enough: Reconnaissance of a foreign power's naval base. But the country is hostile. Details about the op don't make a lot of sense. And don't get him started on his handlers. Battling magic and bureaucracy, Linn penetrates the base, but is discovered. It's going to take every trick he's learned his career to make it home. And if Linn isn't careful, this might be his last mission.

**Available as in eBook, print, Kindle Unlimited, and audio.**

Whitaker Lyon Press is a small publisher located in Broadway, Virginia specializing in anthologies and short story collections.

For updates on new publications and submission calls, subscribe to our newsletter. As a special bonus, new subscribers will receive James Blakey's short story "Do Not Pass Go..." named one of the Best of the Best by SleuthSayers.org.

Website: WhitakerLyon.com
Instagram: whitakerlyonpress
Twitter/X: whitakerlyon

# Read an Excerpt from SUPERSTITION

## A Paranormal Thriller by James Blakey

*A mirror shatters. An umbrella is opened indoors. A black cat crosses your path. All omens of bad luck that no one takes seriously. But at Van Buren University when these and other superstitions are broken, students die.*

***

*Saturday 1:13am*

Her headlamp illuminating the way, the college student trudged to the campfire circle and dumped another armful of sticks and leaves.

Satisfied with the pile, she rested on a boulder, her breath visible in the chilly air as she retrieved a bottle of water. To her right, an Adirondack 46er loomed. Above, a cloudless sky of stars twinkled, no city to drown their light.

Easier to try this at the nature preserve back on campus, but even at this late hour that risked awkward encounters with pot-smoking art majors or insomniac townies.

From her overstuffed green-and-gold backpack, she retrieved half a dozen copies of the college newspaper. She crumpled the pages, placing them strategically amongst the branches, then marinated the heap with charcoal lighter fluid.

She struck a match and tossed it. Orange flames erupted, blinding her for a second, enveloping her in a wave of heat. The hypnotizing fire reminded her of summer camping trips with her father. *Should have brought marshmallows.*

Her phone chimed. Five minutes until the new moon.

She pulled out the shrink-wrapped lamb chops, on sale for $9.99 per pound at Price Chopper. The student wouldn't, couldn't, sacrifice a living animal for the power she craved. Even the thought of touching raw meat filled her disgust. She slipped on a pair of latex gloves liberated from biology lab, then tossed the chops into the flames.

The scent of burning meat filled the air. She hoped to finish before any bears or wolves arrived.

She retrieved the blue textbook, turning to the marked page. Squinting at the diagram, then the sky, she oriented herself, zeroing in on Orion's Belt. A couple of moon widths to the east, she located Alpha Monocerotis.

Of course, that wasn't what the Picts called the star two millennia ago when they ruled what today is Scotland. No one knew their name for it. Almost all their knowledge had been lost. One scrap that survived: their high priestesses worshipped this star for luck.

No bars on her phone. Not a problem. The student pulled the folded printout from her pocket, silently rehearsing the spell. There wasn't a person alive who could reconstruct the enchantment the way the Picts originally spoke it. Her new friends on the dark web assured her that Modern English would work fine, as long as it rhymed.

The past few weeks, she experimented with charms and simple conjuring. Enough to prove to herself that magic was real, and she possessed the power to wield it.

The phone beeped. *Now.*

She stood before the fire, hand raised to the sky, pointing at the faint red star.

The paper rippled in the wind. She focused on the magic, emptying her mind of all other thoughts.

As she recited the words, all feeling receded, as if her consciousness left her physical form behind, merging with the fire, the star, the spell.

> *Goddesses of the Night, hear my plea*
> *Bring Success and Prosperity*
> *My offering to you, a favored sheep*
> *A promise to you, I will always keep*
> *To my endeavors great and small*
> *I call upon you, one and all*
> *With a whisper soft and a heart so true*
> *I conjure Fortune to come anew*
> *Bring me riches, bring me fame*
> *And banish all my doubts and shame*
> *I summon the forces of Star and Sky*
> *To grant me Destiny that cannot die*
> *By my will and desire so strong*
> *This Magic now shall not go wrong*
> *Bringing Luck to my life at last*
> *So mote it be, this Spell is cast.*

She became aware: clothes sticking to her sweat-drenched body, mouth dry, hair plastered to her head, heart pounding. She stumbled to the boulder, resting, regaining her strength.

An owl screeched in the darkness. Good sign? Owls were supposed to be magical. Or was that some Harry Potter nonsense?

The owl quieted. No crickets at this altitude. No sound but the wind and faint jet engines as red-and-green navigation lights hurried across the sky.

The student didn't look or feel different. No supernatural power coursing through her veins. No enhanced perceptions allowing her to observe a secret world. No ethereal light enveloping her.

How anticlimactic. What do you expect for $9.99 a pound?

No way to know if she cast the spell correctly.

No way to test if the magic was working.

No way to tell if this ceremony was a big waste of time.

Not waiting for any predators that caught the scent of the sacrifice, she doused the flames with three bottles of water. Buried the ashes with her collapsible shovel.

*Only you can prevent forest fires.*

She scoured the area, gathering any trash.

*Leave no trace.*

She slipped the pack on her back and began the four-mile hike to the trailhead. She stifled a yawn. At least it was downhill.

Thirty minutes on the trail and her mind was numb. Legs on auto. Step, step, step. Leaves crunching under her feet. Another three miles to go. All she wanted was to get back to her dorm, make a cup of hot cocoa, and crawl into bed.

*Gack!* A spider web across the trail on her face, in her mouth. She spit and raised a hand as the toe of her hiking boot caught a root. She pitched forward, losing her balance, falling toward the sharp rocks on this section of the trail. Arms flailing, she couldn't stop herself. In the darkness, her hand grabbed a branch, wrenching her shoulder, but arresting her fall.

The student righted herself, let out a deep breath, her palm scraped and scratched. Need to be careful. Could have broken a leg or worse. Been stranded with no way to call for help. And no one knew she was up here. Pretty lucky.

A smile spread across her face.

*Pretty lucky.*

"It works!" she shouted into the night.

*** 

SUPERSTITION (Book One of The Secrets of Van Buren University) by James Blakey and published by City Owl Press available as an eBook or in print from your favorite book retailer.